DRAK THE PRINCE

Storm over Vallia is a complete story of the magnificent and mysterious, beautiful and terrible world of Kregen, a planet orbiting Antares four hundred light-years from Earth. On that world of headlong adventure much may be achieved and much lost. Far more than merely a strong sword arm is required for victory. Far more than a cunning and devious brain is needed to secure success.

For Drak, Prince Majister of Vallia, son of Dray Prescot and Delia, emperor and empress of Vallia, and Queen Lushfymi of Lome, passionate, willful, extraordinarily beautiful, mysterious, and Silda Segutoria, daughter of Seg and Thelda Segutorio, are caught in a web of fate and intrigue, of blood and death that demands of them all that they are.

But the story begins with Lon the Knees, animal handler, as, dragged from caring for his domestic animals, he marches in the victory parade of Kov Vodun Alloran, traitorous and usurping master of all Southwest Vallia.

Under the streaming mingled lights of the Suns of Scorpio the fates of these people of Kregen twine among the destinies of that exotic world.

ALAN BURT AKERS

The adventures of Dray Prescot
are narrated in DAW Books:

THE TIDES OF KREGEN
RENEGADE OF KREGEN
KROZAIR OF KREGEN
SEG THE BOWMAN
DELIA OF VALLIA
WEREWOLVES OF KREGEN
WITCHES OF KREGEN
etc.

STORM OVER VALLIA

by

Dray Prescot

As told to Alan Burt Akers

DAW Books, Inc.
Donald A. Wollheim, Publisher
1633 Broadway, New York, N.Y. 10019

PUBLISHED BY
THE NEW AMERICAN LIBRARY
OF CANADA LIMITED

Cover art by Tim Jacobus

DAW Collectors' Book No. 641

First Printing, August 1985

2 3 4 5 6 7 8 9

PRINTED IN CANADA
COVER PRINTED IN U.S.A.

CONTENTS

Chapter One

Lon the Knees

In Vodun Alloran's victory procession the wild beasts, placed ahead of the lines of carts containing trophies and treasure, followed immediately on the heels of the captives. The wild beasts, carefully and expensively gathered, were of many varieties, different of shape and form, of color and physiognomy. One thing they shared in common. They were all hungry.

At the rear of the sweaty reeking mass of savage beasts penned in the cage-carts Lon the Knees marched along sturdily, for all his legs in their bandiness might have circumscribed a barrel—whence his sobriquet. He was of Homo sapiens sapiens stock, clad in rough homespun with decent sandals upon his feet. The long ash stick he carried was more sharply pointed than perhaps the authorities might have allowed in a beast handler, had they known.

"They're restless, bad cess to 'em," said Fandy, walking at Lon's side.

She did not wave her stick at the animal in the cage for which she and Lon were responsible. As a Fristle, a cat-woman, Fandy the Tail's whiskers bristled and her gray-marbled white fur slicked sheening where the universal dust did not coat it in a dull ocher.

"They should have fed them." Lon's nostrils filled with the savage beast smell, thick and clogging. The noise hammering into the bright air made conversation impossible beyond a few paces. "The lord saves money where he should least afford it."

Up ahead squadrons of cavalry rode clearing the way past the mass of onlookers thronging the streets of Rashumsmot, the town having gained greatly in importance since the capital, Rahartium, had been tumbled down into ruin during the wars. Following the wild beasts, bands blared music, and gauzily clad girls, flowers in their hair, flower garlanded, strewed the roadway with petals. Only when all this pomp and pageantry had passed would the high and mighty of the land ride arrogantly along, luxuriating in their wealth and power and prestige.

Fandy the Tail glanced sidelong at Lon, seeing his florid face scowling and paler than usual, the nose still purple but with harsh lines extending downwards to the corners of his mouth, which, uncharacteristically, resembled a snapped rat trap. She was well accustomed to reading facial expressions of other races, as anyone must do who lives on Kregen.

"Lon! You feeling—?"

"Oh, I don't know, Fandy. We're ordinary beast-handlers. I don't care for these monsters. And I suppose I worry over Nol—for a twin brother he's so vastly different from me as to make me wonder at times."

"Twins from different fathers?" Fandy flicked her tail, long and thick and glossy where the dust did not cling. "It's been said. I am not so sure."

The bands played, the people shouted, the soldiers marched, trumpets blew and the beasts penned within their cages paced forward and back, forward and back, bristling.

"Well, Nol went for a mercenary, having the shoulders for a slinger. They took me into the cavalry stables. He fought for our lady the kovneva and when the new kov defeated her—"

"You're here, Lon. He will be all right, you'll see."

"I pray to Opaz that be true. I just feel—by Black Chunguj! I would this damnfool procession was all over!"

The roadway here was ill-paved, cobbles having been ripped out for the catapults, and the wheels of the cage-carts snagged and leaped in the ruts.

Among the gawping crowds Lon was well aware that his friends and acquaintances would be busy. They left the poor folk alone. They dipped the fat and wealthy. It was said Crafty Kando could slide the gold ring off the finger of a woman who'd never taken it off since the day it was placed there. Lon was not a member of the thieves' fraternity. When his work was done and theirs they'd enjoyed good times in one another's company.

In all the shrieking bedlam of bronze gongs, of brass trumpets, of drums and bells, the screams from ahead and the snarls and deep-throated growlings could not be mistaken.

Into that clogging miasma of smells the raw rank taste of blood shocked through like red wine spilled onto a yellow table cloth.

"I knew it!" Lon's face pinched in. He gripped his pointed stick. "I told you so!"

Instantly, Fandy swiveled to glare not up ahead where the bound captives were being slaughtered by the escaped beasts but at their cage. Everything remained battened tight. The latchings, the bolts and bars, were all in place.

Inside the cage the silver-blue unpatterned hide of the churmod reflected light in a ghostly silky-smooth patina. Her blunt head lifted. Her tail thumped once upon the floor of the cage. Languidly, with all the arrogance of a churmod, she lifted on her four rear legs, so that her head, ferocious and deadly, rested still upon her front legs. Two crimson slits regarded Fandy with all the malevolent enmity of any churmod, surly and sadistic and vicious beasts that they are.

Everywhere people were running. The procession broke up, fragmented. Demented with terror, men and women hurled themselves into doorways, clambered up into windows, tried to shin up the pillars to the safety of the balconies where the bright scarves and the flowers and feathers waved still in mockery of the pandemonium below.

The churmod stood up on her eight legs. Eight sets of claws whicked out like razors. Without a sound, the churmod stood there, swaying with the lurchings of the cagecart. In the last moment before the cart stopped, its off fore wheel dropped into a rut. The whole cage tilted, groaning, and remained canted.

The churmod's enormous hissing sounded like a volcano spitting steam.

She hurled herself at the front bars, splintered them through, catapulted out onto the roadway, a lethal silvery-blue phantom of horror.

Fandy the Tail vanished in the opposite direction, the last tip of that fat tail flicking out of sight past a bundle of bandsmen all struggling to rid themselves of their instruments.

The churmod in those long lazily-leaping bounds soared toward the fracas ahead, toward the screams and toward the luscious scent of blood.

Cursing everyone—and Kov Vodun Alloran most of all—Lon the Knees did not give himself time to stop and think. Had he done so he would have followed Fandy the Tail.

He began to run toward the sounds of death.

Just why he was doing this he didn't know; of course, he was scared stiff, of course he was an Opaz-forsaken fool, but he did owe a responsibility for the safety of the churmod. Churmods are amazingly rare and costly beasts. Larger than leems, more treacherous than chavonths, they are highly coveted prizes in the Arena. And rumor had it that Vodun Alloran, the new kov, was intent on introducing all the spectacle of the jikhorkdun, the Arena, the training rings, the barracks, all the gambling and the panoply, into this newly conquered island of Rahartdrin.*

Lon ran on his bandy legs, and his tongue lolled.

Very quickly he came upon the ghastly work of the untamed animals.

Headless bodies, and disembodied heads, arms and legs, a scattering of inward parts, bestrewed the roadway. Some of the animals had stopped to appease their hunger. Others, the more unremittingly hostile, continued in their orgy of slaughter.

There was no sign of Lon's churmod.

Sense slapped back to him like a shower of ice across his face.

By the sweet name of Opaz!

What had he been thinking of!

At once he scuttled across the littered roadway, thankful not to be encountered by a stray leem, or a strigicaw, or anything with sharp teeth and claws, and dived into the black rectangle of an open doorway.

His feet tangled in a body by the doorstep. He caught his balance and glanced down. He frowned.

The body was that of a young woman, a firm, proud young woman, who had been slashed so grievously by giant claws that she must have died almost instantly. She wore black leathers,

*Kov: duke. Kovneva: duchess.—A.B.A.

tightly fitting along slender legs and around a narrow waist, flared as to hip and breast. Her helmet with the brave feathers lay rolled into the angle of the doorway.

She was, Lon saw readily enough, a Warrior Maiden. Her rapier and left-hand dagger had availed her nothing, although the sword was still gripped into her black-gloved right fist.

Thoughtfully, he bent and picked up her dagger. As a mere animal-handler, he could never aspire to wearing a rapier. The dagger, awkward though it might be in his right hand, was still of far finer workmanship and temper of metal than anything he was likely to be able to afford to buy down at the Souk of the Armorers.

The street outside looked something like the aftermath of a battle. Bodies lay everywhere. Blood ran to foul bright clothes and dabble in artfully curled hair. Some of the escaped beasts still roamed looking for fresh victims. The sounds of other animals eating crunched sickeningly into the brightness of the day.

Lon stepped over the dead girl and ventured farther inside, anxious to put a strong door between him and the horrors outside.

Along the short passageway from the front entrance to the inner courtyard he padded. A door stood in each wall, that on the right being closed, that on the left open. He looked over his shoulder before moving to the open door and saw a chavonth putting an inquiring head into the entrance. Lon swallowed. The chavonth, his fur in the familiar blue, gray and black hexagonal pattern, spat in sinister fashion. He braced on his six legs. Treacherous, are chavonths, and Lon knew that this specimen would spring in the next heartbeat.

With a yelp of pure terror he dived past the open door and without hesitation flung the solid wooden door shut.

He stood with his head bowed against the door, shuddering. He was just a simple animal-tender, and so the kov had ordered him, along with others in the same trade, to take charge of his new menagerie. These savage beasts had been gathered from far afield across the seas. Lon was used to ordinary sensible animals, used for pulling carts and ploughs, for riding on, for performing the ordinary sensible tasks demanded by ordinary sensible people.

He was not used to these ferocious assemblages of claws and fangs. No, by Beng Debrant, patron saint of animal husbandry!

A low spitting awful growl from the room at his back stiffened his spine as though he'd been shot through by an arrow.

He wriggled himself around, slowly—slowly!—to stare in appalled horror upon the scene in that downstairs chamber of an unknown house.

The girl clad in black leathers like the poor dead girl in the entranceway snapped: "Stand still, dom!"

Lon the Knees had no intention of doing anything else. Long before he could get the door open the chavonth in the room would be on him. And if he did, the thing's mate waited for him outside.

The sweat ran down his nose and into his eyes and he dare not move. The blue and black and gray hexagons upon the hide of the beast pulsed. He lifted his front left paw and Lon saw the blood glimmering upon it. There was more blood upon the beast's hide, fouling that hexagonal pattern.

There was blood, too, upon the sword in the girl's fist . . .

Lon did not know the name of that sword or of what pattern it might be. It looked something like the common clanxer, the cut and thrust sword of Vallia; but there were differences that even he could see. His brother Nol, now, would probably know. Lon stood and sweated and was thankful he was so bandy his knees could not knock together and so enrage this frightful beast.

Of the details of the room Lon took in absolutely nothing, apart from a vague awareness of a heavy table in the casement window, a few chairs, and the three bodies on the floor. The Warrior Maiden stood with her black-booted feet firmly planted in front of the three corpses.

The twin suns, Zim and Genodras, slanting their mingled streaming light upon the scenes of carnage outside, twinkled in odd refractory reflections of jade and ruby within the shadows of the room. Lon just stood, petrified.

He could feel that both his hands were empty. Now, if he'd kept his long pointed stick. . . . The mere idea of actually trying to push that stick in front of him at the chavonth gave him a dizzy feeling of extreme ill health.

From the time before dawn when the twin suns rose in the sky, Lon had been murkily convinced that this was an evil day. He'd said as much to Nath the Goader, an intemperate and ill-humored fellow at the best of times. Nath, in charge of the wild animals and worried out of his wits by the unwelcome responsibility, had merely growled in his beard and sent Lon off with a flea in his ear, or, as Kregans say, a zorca hoof up the rump. The truth of Lon's premonitions was here, awfully here, in this savage chavonth, and the corpses, and the blood, and the shambles outside. . . .

The girl's downdrawn level gaze did not waver from the chavonth.

When the thing launched itself into its lethal leap, she would be ready. Lon knew that. It was evident in every line of her body, every vibrant inch that, he saw with suddenly uncluttered eyes, was of extraordinary beauty.

Her sword did not waver.

Her left arm was held at her back, the hand hidden.

She was a Jikai Vuvushi, a Battle Maiden, and she had been riding with the cavalry at the head of the procession. No doubt these three poor corpses, all men, with the girl at the entranceway, had been also with the advance guard. They'd spurred back to find out what the trouble was and had encountered horror.

So now this girl, this Jikai Vuvushi, faced the terror alone.

Lon swallowed again and slowly began to draw

his right hand down to the awkward hilt of the main gauche thrust through his belt. Something about this girl attracted him in ways he was too wise to encourage. She was not for him. He tumbled the girls in the taverns when he could, and joyed in that. This girl possessed an aura, a flickering flame of power and allure, and she was tough. No doubt of that. She was battle-hardened.

The blood along the chavonth's flank matching the blood on her blade proved that.

The chavonth sprang.

The girl leaped aside with such grace, such beauty of movement that the breath caught in Lon's throat.

As she leaped and so avoided the long slashing stroke from the beast's front claws, she struck. Her sword scored all along the animal's fore sixth. She span about, sword blurring up for another stroke and the chavonth backed off, spitting.

"By Vox!" she said, viciously disappointed. And still her left hand remained invisibly at her back.

The hunting cat showed no interest in the three bodies on the floor. He glared from hating, slit eyes upon the living breathing form of the girl. And, again, he lifted one front paw, the claws sharp and curved and shining.

A scratching began on the door, and a hideous meowling. The other chavonth, mate to that one penned here, sought entrance. Lon felt his famous knees giving way; but still his right hand dropped cautiously lower and lower to the hilt of the left-hand dagger.

With the sudden and ferocious changes of fortune that overtake anyone who lives on the world of Kregen, the noise outside the door changed. The chavonth's scratching ceased. The mewling screeched into a spitting snarl. Mingled with that noise another noise penetrated, a long ominous hissing.

Whether or not chavonths, or any other of the many and varied life forms represented by Kregen's savage fauna, could communicate with one another, Lon didn't as yet know. But the noise outside the door was easily understood within the room.

That low evil hissing was the churmod—Lon's churmod for which he was responsible to the lord. In the next heartbeat it was all over. The snarling uproar ceased on a long screech of agony. No sound of the chavonth remained. Then, again, low and demonic, the hissing of the churmod.

What happened then Lon could not afterward well remember. His hand reached the dagger hilt and he drew ready to throw. He ranked himself as a man who could throw a knife, even one so clumsy as this left-hand dagger.

The chavonth, distraught at the death of his mate, for he had read those bestial sounds outside the door as accurately as the humans, whicked his tail and leaped.

Lon hurled the dagger.

He saw the point go into a blue patterned hexagon. He was aware of the girl's sword sliding up and then he blinked in the abrupt blinding wink of fire, he caught a blurred impression of steel slashing, of the brilliance of the emerald and ruby suns light glancing off polished metal. The girl swung back and the sword licked again. The chavonth reeled about spouting blood, half its muzzle ripped away. One eye dangled. It screamed. The Jikai Vuvushi, very assured, very calm, stepped forward and drove her sword deeply into the beast's side. That blade, Lon knew, and trembled, had burst through the savage heart and stilled its beating forever.

Strangely, without speaking, the girl turned her back on Lon the Knees. A brown canvas strap and sack thumped against her side. She swung about to face him, the sword dripping red in her fist.

She spoke evenly enough, yet lightly, on a breath, as though the horror of the past moments had not been so easily disposed of in the thrust of a sword.

"I give you my thanks, dom. Your name?"

"Why, my lady—it is Lon the Knees—"

"Yes."

And she smiled. And Lon the Knees was overwhelmed.

He licked his lips and swallowed and got out: "My lady! You have slain a chavonth! It is a great jikai!"

He would not dare, naturally, to ask her name in return.

Her smile did not falter.

"A little jikai, perhaps, Lon the Knees. To gain the great jikai, let along the High Jikai, one must do far more than this. Far more."

He opened his mouth, and she went on: "Now give me a hand with this young lord. His companions are dead, which is unfortunate for them, although no doubt somewhere in this land of Rahartdrin someone is giving thanks to Opaz for this eventuality."

Lon didn't follow all this; but he stepped across, knees trembling, and helped to raise up one of the corpses.

This body was clad in gorgeous clothes of a nature that, while they filled Lon with envy, filled him also with repugnance.

As though inconsequentially, she said: "You throw a cunning knife, Lon."

"Aye, my lady."

"It did the trick. Gave me time—hold his arm, the idiot keeps on falling over—now, you young lord, open your damned eyes!" She slapped the corpse around the face and, lo!, the corpse's eyes opened.

"Help!" The puffy lips shook as the man screamed.

The girl shook his shoulder. "It is all over! You are safe, Jen* Cedro."

This young lord Cedro in the foppish gaudy clothes took some time to calm down. He was sick. His eyes, of a pale transparency so unlike the normal deep Vallian brown, stared vacantly at the room, the dead chavonth, his two dead companions. He shuddered and vomited again.

*Jen: Vallian for lord. Notor is Havilfarese. Pantor is Pandahemic.—A.B.A.

Only now, this close to the girl as he helped with this petulant young lord, was Lon aware of the blood scored along the rip in her black leathers. The slash from razor-sharp claws bloodied her left shoulder. That, Lon surmised was why she'd held her left hand at her back.

"My lady! You are hurt—"

"A scratch. As soon as I've handed Jen Cedro over I'll have the needle lady attend to it."

"At least let me bind it up—"

"Don't fuss, Lon the Knees."

He felt chastened, and so said no more.

"That damned churmod is still prowling about outside." She sounded fretful and just as savage as the damned churmod. "I don't fancy having to go up against her with—"

"My lady! That would be madness!"

"Oh, aye, by Vox, absolute madness. So I won't."

"Thank the good Opaz!"

"We'll sit tight in here and wait until Kov Vodun sorts out the whole stupid mess. You can tell me about yourself."

So he told her, not that there was much to tell. Orphaned at an early age and sent to work on a farm, been looking after animals all his life. His twin brother, Nol, gone for a mercenary slinger and who might have any sobriquet now, a source of ever-present foreboding.

"Why, Lon?"

"Soldiers get themselves killed, my lady."

"Oh, aye, they do that. But then, so do beast-handlers who don't know their job."

"My lady!" Lon was aware of deep disappointment that he should not have felt. The great ones of the land would always blame someone other than themselves. "I am not trained to handle wild beasts—give me a Quoffa, or a mytzer, a zorca or—"

"I know, Lon. I am not blaming you. Far from it."

"They should not have put the captives so near the wild beasts, and—"

"And the cages were ludicrous. Yes, I guessed that. But, Lon the Knees, do you not think it strange that so many wild animals escaped—all at once?"

"I saw the churmod break the bars. It was frightening."

"Assuredly. Yet I suspect that a hand loosened the bars of the cages—not yours, Lon, believe me, I did not intend to mean that."

Oddly enough, given his usual attitude to the high and mighty of the world, Lon believed her, believed she spoke the truth. She was, he could see, a most remarkable young lady.

"You do not ask my name, Lon."

"That is beyond my reach, my lady, as you know."

"Oh—I see. Yes. I am a Jikai Vuvushi and am used to rough ways. Well then, Lon the Knees, I am Lyss the Lone—well, that is one name by which I am known."

Very gravely, Lon said: "Llahal and Lahal, Lyss the Lone. Now we have made pappattu properly."

"Lahal, Lon."

So the introductions were made.

Lord Cedro groaned and started to roll over so Lyss the Lone pushed him away to avoid his own vomit.

Added to the rank smell of blood in the chamber the sour stink of Cedro's sick gave Lon a queasy sensation, he who was used to the stenches of a farmyard!

Lyss walked to the window and looked out. She shook her head.

"The beasts still stalk arrogantly. There is no sign of a human being—alive, that is."

"Oh," said Lon.

"The kov will be rounding up his people now. Pretty soon they'll come back and try to round up the beasts—"

"I should be there to help them."

"You will stay here and help me."

"Quidang,* my lady."

"So you never wanted to go for a mercenary, then?"

"Oh, I went off with my brother Nol. They took him for a slinger; me they sent home, laughing. But I was in one army for a time, looking after the totrixes."

"Someone has to, otherwise the army would not ride."

Nervously, trading on this amazing friendship he sensed between them, Lon ventured: "And you, my lady. You have been in many famous battles?"

*Quidang: An acknowledgment that the hearer will obey an order. "Very good!" Mainly used by military.—A.B.A.

"Some."

"A —I see . . ."

"A battle is a battle, Lon. A messy business."

"Yes, my lady."

The idea that a battlefield was not exactly the right place for a young lady could only occur to Lon the Knees, or any of his contemporaries, as it might apply to one particular girl, one prized loved one. Girls had always fought in battles, and the Jikai Vuvushi regiments were justly feared.

Lon was perfectly content, now, to sit tight in this chamber and wait for Kov Vodun to come for them. That the kov would come, Lon felt no doubt. Now he knew this young and unpleasant lord was Jen Cedro, he knew him to be one of Kov Vodun's nephews. If the foppish idiot was valued by his uncle, then rescue would not be long delayed. Thus reasoned Lon the Knees.

Also, and in this Lon felt unsure, he would meet the kov, face to face. Vodun Alloran might lord it over wide lands; the common folk could hope to see him barely more than a handful of times during their lives. The great ones of the earth rode past in a glitter of gold amid the trumpets and banners; the common herd cheered from the crowds and saw only what the dazzlement in their eyes allowed.

Assured that Cedro was still alive, Lyss the Lone did not seem bothered that he relapsed into unconsciousness. She sat on one of the chairs twisted to face the windows. She sat still and trim in her black leathers, and Lon felt the pang strike through him. If only . . . !

Well, jolly fat Sendra down at The Leather Bottle had been kind to him in the past, and he could always shut his eyes and dream. . . .

Noise and fresh uproar in the street told that at last rescue had arrived. The clatter of hooves, the screeching fury of wild beasts skewered and feathered, the high yells of men and women drunk on slaying, filtered in through the window. Lyss stood up. She hitched her rapier and main gauche around, picked up her other sword, solid and powerful, and started for the door.

"My lady!" Lon was alarmed to such an extent he scared himself at the intensity of his own feelings.

"Well?"

"You cannot—I mean—why go out now?"

"I am a Jikai Vuvushi."

Lon stiffened his spine.

"Aye! And like to be a dead one if you go outside that door now—my lady."

Thankfully, she did not say: "And you would care?" Such banality, they both recognized, had long since vanished between them. She smiled that dazzling smile.

"I believe your justified concern no longer applies—listen!"

From outside the door the sounds of the churmod's death hissed in, and Lon had no difficulty visualizing the hail of bolts from the crossbows, sleeting in to shred and bloody that ghostly silvery-blue hide.

Lyss opened the door.

"Hai! The lord Cedro is here, unharmed. Hurry, famblys, and take him up carefully, for he is beloved of the lord kov."

Men and women wearing a variety of colorful uniforms entered the room, and at once began to attend to Cedro. Lon stared at the open doorway.

Vodun Alloran, Kov of Kaldi, conqueror of this island of Rahartdrin, entered. Lon stared, fascinated, quite unaware of his own peril in thus staring so openly at a great lord.

Alloran looked the part. His clothes were sumptuous, for he no longer wore the normal Vallian buff tunic and breeches; golden wire, lace, feathers and fol-de-rols smothered him in magnificence. His shrewd, weatherbeaten face contained harshness engraved as a habit, and the bright brown Vallian eyes, partially hidden by down-drooping lids, revealed a little of the fury of ambition seething within him.

He wore an aigrette, the feathers of maroon and gray, the colors of Kaldi, and the golden device that of a leaping sea-barynth, a long and sinuous monster of Kregen's seas. His own personal retainers wore sleeves banded in maroon and gray in the old style of Vallia. He stared about from under those drooping eyelids, and Lon abruptly switched his gaze to Lyss.

She stood, upright and slim in her black leathers.

"My nephew," said the kov. "He is unharmed?"

"He is well, my lord kov, praise be to Opaz—"

"Yes. He would escape from a pack of leems without a rent in his coat."

Lyss said nothing. Lon stood with his tongue cleaving to the roof of his mouth.

Alloran stared about with that aloof, disdainful look of the great ones of the world.

"There has been a mischief done here," he said. He spoke through his teeth. "And I will have the guilty ones hung by their heels over the battlements until they are shredded to bone."

Watching Lyss the Lone, Lon saw the way she held herself, the tautness of her, the poise. Was that a fine trembling along her limbs, the ghost of a twitch of muscle in her cheek? He'd conceived the instant idea that this glorious girl feared nothing. She had faced and overcome a savage wild beast, not even claiming a jikai for the deed. Now she stood watchful, like a falcon poised ready to take flight, alert and wary.

Naturally Lon stood in awe and fear of Kov Vodun Alloran.

But did this Battle Maiden, this superb Jikai Vuvushi, stand in fear of the kov?

No. No, Lon the Knees could not believe that this girl feared anything in Kregen.

Chapter Two

Of the concerns of Drak, Prince Majister of Vallia

The battle was lost a half an hour after it began with the totally unexpected appearance of a second hostile army swarming up from the sand dunes on the left flank. The Vallians broke and fled.

The First Army, commanded by Drak, Prince Majister of Vallia, trudged dispiritedly back from that disastrous field. Then the rain fell.

Jumbled regiments on foot slogged through mud that thickened and stuck like glue. A few artillery pieces saved from the ruin, ballistae and catapults swathed in coarse sacking against the rain, struggled on drawn by a motley collection of animals, and by men. The cavalry, who had suffered grievously, walked their animals, and everywhere heads hung down.

The wounded, those who could be collected, were transported in improvised fashion, for the supply of ambulance carts proved woefully insufficient.

Sliding, slipping, dragging themselves through the mud, the First Army staggered on eastwards across the imperial province of Venavito in southwest Vallia.

Jiktar Endru Vintang led his zorca through the mud, holding the bridle so that he walked to the side, for the zorca's single spiral horn jutting from his forehead could inflict a nasty nudge if anyone was foolish enough to walk directly in front of so superb an animal. His saddle dripped water, and his orderly would spit brickdust cleaning up the weaponry strapped both to zorca and Endru.

The long lines of men and animals kept doggedly on in the rattle of the rain and the gruesome footing.

Jiktar Endru commanded one of the prince's personal bodyguard regiments.*

He was three-quarters of the way up the ladder of promotions within the Jiktar rank, and hoped soon to make Chuktar. With this disastrous Battle of Swanton's Bay to ruin their plans, Endru morosely felt that promotions for anyone were a long way away. You'd have to take the place of a dead superior and soldier on in your own grade for a bit yet. That was his surmise.

*The four main ranks in most Kregan armies are: Deldar, commander of ten. Hikdar, pastang or company, or squadron commander. Jiktar, regimental commander. Chuktar, general. A Chuktar is selected as Kapt, commander in chief.—A.B.A.

Nobody talked. They all went sloshing on in a profound and gloomy silence, broken by the slash of the rain, the creaking of axle wheels, the suck and splash of feet in mud, and the groans of the wounded. All these distressing sounds faded within the bitterness of the silence engulfing the army.

Endru Vintang ti Vandayha, tough as old boots, efficient, a superb zorcaman, a warrior who understood discipline and let his regiment know he understood, had fought as a Freedom Fighter in Valka, and counted himself supremely lucky to be selected by the Prince Majister to command the bodyguard regiment called the Prince Majister's Sword Watch.* The best part was that, feeling a real and powerful affection for the prince, Endru knew that Prince Drak liked and trusted him and treated him as a friend.

He knew he felt as many and many a poor wight in this defeated army felt. He felt they'd let Prince Drak down badly, very badly indeed.

But, still and all! That second army, suddenly appearing over the sand dunes where scouts had reported nothing apart from shellfish and crabs! That had been the stunner.

Those Opaz-forsaken Kataki twins had been the cause of this defeat. That seemed certain.

Glimmering spectrally through the slanting rain a light appeared ahead. Wearily, Endru flapped

*ti: "of" indicating the holder as a person of some substance in the locality or town. Of as "na" or "nal" indicated persons of higher rank and greater estates—A.B.A.

back the cloth over his saddle and with a soft word to Dapplears, his zorca, stuck a leg over and mounted up. Even then, quick as he was, he sat in wetness and felt the discomfort through his breeches. One thing was for sure in all the surrounding desolation; this uniform was ruined beyond repair.

He nudged Dapplears, for no true zorcaman put spurs to so fiery and spirited a saddle animal, and walked him up alongside his regiment.

"Deldar Fresk! Ten men with me. *Bratch!*"

Eleven of them, they rode out ahead of that bedraggled rout toward the light which Endru knew to be shining in a window of a house in the little village of Molon. He said nothing, did not turn his head, as he passed the powerful figure walking sturdily beside his zorca at the head of the column. The prince would be in no mood for polite conversation now, by Vox!

The inhabitants of the village, apprised by that seemingly magical dissemination of country news, had fled.

There were beds for the wounded, and roofs for a fair number of those fortunate enough to cram into the little houses. There was even a little food. Fires were lit and clothing began to steam, filling the close confined atmosphere with that particular charring, moist, fibrous smell of drying clothes. When he had seen to his duties, Endru reported to the prince.

"They'll get some rest for the night, jis," he said, using the "jis" as the shortened form of majister, for Prince Drak did not care to be addressed as majister. He was not too keen on the slightly more formal 'majis' although that was how most of those not in his immediate circle addressed him.

"And those we have left on the field will sleep even more profoundly." Drak sounded depressed.

"The odds were more than two to one, nearer three to one. Had we not—"

"Run off?"

"Aye, jis! Had we not done so, many more of us would sleep on the field this night. And then, what of the morrow?"

"You are right, Endru. We must look to tomorrow."

Endru was of an age with the prince. He felt perfectly confident in his ability to be allowed to say: "Bitterness over this defeat, jis, will avail us nothing. Those damned Kataki twins wrought the mischief, I'll be bound."

"I did not see them in the fight. Did you?"

"No."

Drak sat himself down on a rough wooden seat and put his forearms on the scrubbed table top. The fire threw harsh shadows into his face. Yet Endru could see the power there, the arrogant beak of a nose, the jut of chin, all the charisma he possessed, shared and inherited from his father the emperor. They were much alike, yet Prince Drak for all his austere ways, his uprightness, his dedication to his duty, possessed a streak of more gentle character from his mother, the divine Empress Delia.

The small cottage room contained other men

and women, Kapt Enwood nal Venticar, the prince's right-hand man and his chief of staff, crusty old Jiktar Naghan the Bow, commanding the prince's bodyguard regiment, the Prince Majister's Devoted Archers, his personal servants, one or two of the sutlers come to report the damage, various people who had business with the prince, and Chuktar Leone Starhammer, commanding Queen Lushfymi's regiment of Jikai Vuvushis. Now Kapt Enwood resumed the conversation Endru's entrance had interrupted.

"Jiktar Endru confirms my view, then, jis. I am confident the Kataki twins commanded. It is certain that Vodun Alloran was not there."

"The quicker he is put down, the better it will be for Vallia."

"Yet he is clever and resourceful. He commands many men. And he's getting his gold from somewhere—"

"Aye!" burst out Drak. "But where?"

"It is my view," put in Leone Starhammer, "there is sorcery involved here."

No one cared to answer that. This Leone, a full-bodied woman, plain of face, dark of hair, with biceps that could smash a sword through oak, kept herself and her girls up to a very high fighting pitch. Fortunately, in Drak's mind as in the others', the Jikai Vuvushis had not been heavily engaged during the short fray.

"Let's have the maps out and see what we can cobble together and call a plan."

Again Endru felt that stab of dismay at the depths of the prince's despondency.

The maps were brought and spread upon the table and the people gathered about them in the light of a lamp, a cheap mineral oil lamp.

Drak began by stating the obvious.

"We are fighting for Vallia. The whole island empire has been broken into pieces, and slavers and slave masters, villains who batten on our misery, have swarmed in to ravage and despoil. We will not allow slavery in Vallia. We will not allow honest folk to be crushed into the mud. So we fight for them. And, this day, we have been defeated."

"Tomorrow, jis," said Kapt Enwood, "or the day after or the day after that, we will be victorious."

"And how many days must the downtrodden wait for us?"

"As many as the Invisible Twins made manifest in the glory of Opaz decide, my prince."

Drak took that well enough. He stabbed a finger at the map.

"At least, they did not pursue their victory."

"I lost the better part of a fine totrix brigade," said Kapt Enwood, grimly. "Then the rains came." He drew a breath. "No. They did not pursue."

Where Drak had stabbed his so savage finger the little bay, known as Swanton's Bay, gouged a piece out of the Venavito coastline. To the east lay the province of Delphond, the Garden of Vallia. Delphond was the province of the Empress Delia. The people were languid and easy-going, joying in the good things of life which they produced so profusely from their lovely land, not easily aroused. During the Time of Troubles they had changed. From slitting the throats of stragglers in ditches, they now sent many strapping sons and daughters to swell the ranks of the regular Vallian army. Delphond was cut off from many direct routes and canal trunk systems, and invasions usually passed the province by. Drak did not wish to contemplate what his mother would say if he allowed invading hordes once more to ravage her lands.

Northward lay the vadvarate of Thadelm, mostly occupied by Vodun Alloran's mercenaries. There was some resistance to his schemes there, though, and a small force watched the borders.

To the west the kovnate of Ovvend was now once more solidly in Alloran's grip. Ovvend was on the small size for a kovnate province; it was undeniably rich.

West of Ovvend lay the diamond-shaped kovnate of Kaldi, Vodun Alloran's own province. The westerly point of land was the last on the mainland of Vallia. Beyond that extended many islands, chief of which was Rahartdrin, with Tezpor to the north. No word had been received from these islands, or those further west, for many seasons, and spies sent in did not return.

Two divisional commanders had been killed in the battle, so the council was thin on the ground. Brigadiers would have to be appointed to take over the divisions; as Endru had suspected, they would not advance a grade within the Chuktar rank.

"I am determined to hold them on this line," said Drak, indicating a river some miles to the east. "We must draw them north."

He was aware that these people, all well-meaning, gathered here to help and advise, would know why he wanted to do that. The thought of Delphond once more put to the torch and the sword made him limp with anger. He had spent some of his childhood there and he loved Delphond's lazy ways, her soft rivers, the winding dusty lanes, the fields of fruit and hop gardens, the fat ponshos with fleeces as white as the clouds above. Oh, no, he must draw Alloran's army, commanded by the Kataki twins, toward the north where they could be entrapped in mountains.

Kapt Enwood said: "We shall have to send to Vondium to ask for reinforcements. I see no alternative."

"They are short of troops in the capital."

"If you appeal to the emperor—"

Drak's head snapped up. Almost, almost, he burst out: "Ask my father? Oh, yes, we'll ask him. But he won't be there. He never is. He'll be off gallivanting around the world doing derring deeds, hurtling under the Suns in his scarlet breechclout and swinging his Krozair longsword. Oh, yes, ask the emperor, an' you please. Much good will it do you."

Instead, he said: "Send and ask, Kapt."

"Quidang!"

Their faces harshly highlighted by lamp and the fire, they thrashed out some kind of plan. They would draw the enemy on, try to chivvy him northwards, get him in unfriendly country, continuously ambush him, run him ragged. They could not stand up to a face to face set-piece battle. Not while they were now, having sustained casualties, at a worse ratio than one to three. When the reinforcements marched and flew in, why, then, with the blessing of Opaz and the strength and cunning of Vox, they'd knock Vodun Alloran's teeth down his throat.

And his two whip-tailed Katakis with him, too . . .

"We must preserve the Phalanx intact," said Drak, stating the essential and the obvious. "Without them at Swanton's Bay we would have been destroyed."

"Aye, jis."

"Get the kervaxes moving at first light and withdraw the entire Phalanx force to the east. We will need light infantry for ambush work, and light cavalry."

They talked on for a space, settling details, then at Drak's suggestion, they retired to try to sleep for what was left of the night. The rain continued. The sky was a mere black platter pressing down on the land. Leone Starhammer lingered.

"Jis?"

"Yes, Leone?"

"The queen—I fear she will take this news ill."

"She will have to be told, I suppose. . . ."

"Jiktar Shirl the Elegant fell today—"

"I am desolated! I did not know."

"A stray varter bolt pierced her through the

throat, above the corselet rim. She died in my arms." Leone's hard plain face revealed no outward emotion; Drak was not deceived.

"She was handmaid to the queen; but she kept on pestering to go with the army and be a Jikai Vuvushi. In the end the queen relented and gave her assent. Shirl the Elegant was very dear to the queen."

"I see. Then she will have to know. I give thanks to Opaz that the queen stays in Vondium."

Leone stared at him, and the slight movement of her right eyebrow was of enormous significance.

"I believe the queen would dearly love to be with the army, to march with her regiment of Jikai Vuvushis, to be with the man she—the prince she—"

"All right, Leone. I know, you know, the whole damned world of Kregen knows Queen Lushfymi of Lome wants to marry me. Well, I am not so sure."

"May I say, prince, that it would be a splendid match? Lome is a very rich country, and Pandahem is allied to us now, after the wars, and—"

"Allied to us! By Vox, Leone! You saw that fresh damned army come shrieking off the beaches! They were from Pandaheem. They were Pandaheem. I wouldn't be surprised if there weren't more than a few men from Lome among 'em!"

"Majister!"

"Aye, and a few girls, too!"

"Jis—you do me dishonor—I cannot—"

Before Drak had time to spit out that he didn't really mean what he said in the heat of angry resentment, Leone fled from the room. Drak swore. He swept the maps off the table, then he kicked the table leg, then he swore some more.

Women!

The trouble was ever since Queen Lush—at once he mentally corrected himself. He ought to refer to her as Queen Lushfymi, although she was generally known as Queen Lush. She'd come to Vallia to marry the old emperor, Drak's grandfather, and when he had been killed Queen Lush, after some fraught experiences with sorcery, had decided her best bet would be to marry the Prince Majister. One day Prince Drak would be the emperor.

Well, and so he would, if his father had his way. Drak refused even to think about all that. He had a campaign to run and Vodun Alloran, the damned traitor, to whack. Time enough later to think of marrying.

And then—of course!—he could not stop himself thinking of Silda.

Daughter of his father's boon companion, Seg Segutorio, the finest Bowman of Loh in the world of Kregen, Silda Segutoria troubled Drak in ways he just couldn't fathom. He knew she loved him. She had risked her life, willingly offering it up, to save him from death. She was marvelous, wonderful, impetuous, quicksilver, and damned devious, too, like all the women who were members of the famous if secret sorority the Sisters of the Rose.

Into the bargain he knew that Seg Segutorio, who was like an uncle to Drak, and his father the emperor and his mother the empress, all wanted

Drak and Silda to marry. That seemed in their eyes to be inevitable and wonderfully apt.

And here was Queen Lush, sophisticated, alluring, a woman of the world, sensual and clever and reputed possessed of some sorcerous powers, setting her cap at him.

It was all a muddle.

He glanced at his own great Krozair longsword standing in the corner by the fireplace. The coals were mostly burned through now and he'd better turn in before the room became too cold. He was a Krozair of Zy, a member of that martial and mystical Order. Yes, life was a lot simpler out there in the Eye of the World, the inner sea of Kregen. Out there, where his brother Zeg was King of Zandikar, life was simple. If anything wore green you killed it. If anything wore red you fought for it with your life.

As for Silda Segutoria—where in a Herrelldrin Hell had the girl got herself? Where the blazes could she be? She might be in Vondium, where Queen Lush was no doubt living a life of luxury. She might be off on a wild adventure for the Sisters of the Rose. There was a strong possibility she could be with his sister Dayra, or his mother, the Empress Delia, although recent letters had not mentioned her. She could, even, be haring off into breathtaking adventures with his father, the Emperor of Vallia.

Thoroughly dissatisfied, Drak rolled himself up in his cloak and drifted off to sleep where he dreamed dreams of men with no eyes sloshing about in the bloodied surf of Swanton's Bay.

Chapter Three

The kov who would be king

The loss of so many fine specimens was not to be allowed to interfere with the festivities—not if Kov Vodun Alloran na Kaldi had anything to say, no, by Vox!

"There are captives aplenty," he shouted at his chamberlains. "Use them! Do I have to think of everything?"

In preparation for the many ceremonies the streets were garlanded, tapestries and carpets hung down from balconies, ales and wines were brought in by the cartful, trees were decorated with strings of colored lights for the evening entertainments.

Strolling players, whose numbers had declined during the Times of Trouble, were now reappearing. If folk believed that these new troublous times were over, then they could be encouraged in that belief. Troupes of actors and actresses, singers, jugglers, fire-eaters, animal-tricksters, gathered in the town to add their color and sparkle to the festive occasion.

In the natural course of his own estimation of himself, Alloran took his personal tailor on his travels. This functionary shared quarters, meals and salary with the hairdresser, the bootmaker, the perfumer, the mistress of the linen and other men and women whose sole function in life was to care for the person of Vodun Alloran.

"I want clothes more beautiful, more sumptuous, more glorious than any seen before," Alloran instructed his tailor, a snuffily little Och called Opnar the Silk.

"It shall be done, my lord kov," gabbled Opnar.

"After all," said Alloran, looking at himself in the tall mirror in the angle of the room, "after all, this is the first time I have been crowned king." He smiled widely at his own reflection, pleased with the air of authority and regal command he himself sensed emanating from his reflection. "Although I am completely persuaded it will not be the last."

"Assuredly not, my lord kov."

The little Och bid his assistants bring in bales of materials so that a beginning could be made on the choice of fabrics. He was pleased in one way that the kov spoke to him in so familiar a fashion, and in another trembled lest inadvertently a great state secret should slip out and necessitate the removal of his head from his narrow shoulders.

Alloran expressed dissatisfaction with everything he was shown, which was perfectly normal. Opnar did not take out his own fears and ill humor on his assistants. He was in general a gentle man who just wanted to make fine clothes.

"And let there be a great quantity of gold," declared Alloran, forcefully. "Gold lace, gold bullion, gold leaf, gold everywhere. The people must see and know how great a king I am."

That seemed a perfectly logical request and desire to Opnar the Silk. He bobbed and nodded and unrolled more cloth.

A sentry at the double doors bellowed: "Kapt Logan Lakelmi, my lord kov, desires admittance."

Naturally Alloran had installed himself in the finest residence in the town and already plans fomented in his head to increase the size of the place, and build higher walls and more sumptuous chambers. Once he had decided where in his new realms he would build his capital and palace, he would indulge himself in a frenzy of building on a colossal scale.

He gestured negligently with a beringed finger, the sentry vanished to reappear with Kapt Logan Lakelmi.

"My lord kov!" rapped out Lakelmi, saluting.

"Kapt Logan. The news?"

"Is good. The Kataki Strom has gained a great victory over the Prince Majister. A place called Swanton's Bay. The Vallians run in route, and—"

"Hold, Kapt Logan! Yes, the news is excedngly good. The Kataki Strom has done well, although I sent him a great reinforcement for his army. But, Kapt Logan, softly. We are all Vallians in Vallia, although you are a mercenary from Loh, do not forget that. When I am king over all, when I am emperor, I shall be the Emperor of Vallia."

"Yes, my lord kov."

"Vallia!" breathed Alloran. There was genuine emotion in him, his eyes bright. "Yes, I shall be Emperor of Vallia, and Vallians will rule in their own country as is proper." He glanced under down-drawn lids at Lakelmi. "But I shall not forget loyal servants, Kapt Logan. You will not be forgotten."

"I thank you. Do you wish to see the lists—?"

"Later."

Kapt Logan Lakelmi, with the red hair of Loh, with his spare, tall, erect figure, looked every inch the fighting man. Now he acted as Alloran's chief of staff, and longed for an independent command. That would come, he felt sure. The kov's plans encompassed many more campaigns and battles, and there would be employment for many mercenaries for seasons to come.

Lakelmi knew something of Alloran's history. The kov, despairing of ever being kov in those peaceful days before the Times of Troubles, when his father was set to live, it seemed, forever, had gone abroad. He had become a mercenary as a very young man. Then he had worked and fought his way up to become a paktun, a mercenary with a reputation. The next step had been to mort-paktun, a warrior elected by his peers, who wore the silver mortil-head on its silk ribbons at his throat. His fame had spread among his own kind. Before he had taken the next step, to become a zhan-paktun, wearing the golden zhantilhead at his throat, tribulations and disaster had fallen upon Vallia.

Alloran, returning home, his father killed by malignant hostiles, had fought for his kovnate, and lost, and fled to the capital of the country, Vondium.

There he had joined the new Vallian army and, given a brigade by the new emperor, had fought well. He had been selected to go to the southwest with an army and to clear out the slavers and all those festering upon the misery of Vallia, and to return all those provinces to the empire.

Just how the corrosive ambition had at last broken through, Lakelmi was not sure. What was certain was that Vodun Alloran had rejected loyalty to the emperor. He had fought for his own kovnate province, had won that back, had taken neighboring provinces, and then declared his own independence.

The next inevitable step was to crown himself King of Southwest Vallia.

With the latest victory against the forces of the Prince Majister of Vallia to crown his efforts, nothing appeared to stand in his way. His ambitions would be rewarded.

Yes, Kapt Logan Lakelmi felt convinced a bright and prosperous future lay ahead.

That was—if he didn't get himself killed in some stupid affray.

The golden glitter of the pakzhan at his throat on its silken cords told everyone that he was a zhan-paktun. That lofty eminence within the mercenary fraternity was to Logan Lakelmi of far greater importance than his present position as Kapt to Kov Vodun.

Now he pushed the rolled lists back under his left arm. Later, the kov said. Well, that suited Lakelmi.

"Jen," he said. "There is a matter of the runaway slaves who have been recaptured—"

"That is a matter for the judiciary, Logan."

"Assuredly. But I would like to offer them the chance to enroll in the ranks. We do need men."

Alloran scowled.

"Men! They cost gold, you pay them, and sometimes they fight and sometimes they run away. And they get killed and where is the gold then?"

Lakelmi remained silent. Opnar held a roll of watered green silk in his hands, unmoving.

"Slaves who show how ungrateful they are by running away must be punished. I hew to the old traditions of Vallia. Slavery is an institution hallowed by age. I could not live in the new Vallia created by the emperor where he has abolished slavery. The man is a fool, there is no denying that."

"Yes, my lord kov."

"After they have been punished, after they have been striped jikaider you may attempt to recruit them."

"Thank you, my lord kov."

Already schemes jumped into his head. He'd have a private word or three with the Whip-Deldars. They would not stripe the slaves badly, and certainly he'd avoid jikaidering them, a savage punishment in which a left-handed and a right-handed lash criss-crossed their backs with a checkerboard of blood. He'd get himself some prime flint-fodder, by Hlo-Hli!

Then Alloran said with a smile of great craftiness: "But, good Logan, who is to pay the rightful owners of the slaves? Always assuming they do not wish the return of their rightful property."

This emphasis on the rightfulness of it disturbed Lakelmi.

"I will speak to them, my lord kov, and see what may be done."

"Do that, Logan, do that."

"The fact remains, we still need more numbers to fill the ranks of the armies."

"Yes, and I suppose those lists you hold so tightly under your arm tell me of more gold lost with the men of Strom* Rosil's army?"

"Casualties were light—"

"Thank Takar for that!"

"A fresh recruitment should land this afternoon, the argenters have been sighted sailing in without trouble and if each ship carries three hundred men there should be at least six thousand or so."

Lakelmi had deliberately changed the subject of conversation from Strom Rosil. Lakelmi knew that the Kataki Strom had provided most of the gold for the army fighting on the mainland. No one knew where the gold came from; they knew where it went, though, by Lohako the Bold!

*Strom: a rank of nobility equating with count.—A.B.A.

"I hope," grunted Alloran in his offensive way, "there are good fighting men amongst them. We have enough of these mewling weaklings you call flint-fodder."

"That is so, my lord kov."

"And I need first-class cavalry. And air!" He glared at the Kapt. "What I would give for some aerial cavalry, and squadrons of fliers, airboats, to give me mastery aloft. As it is, every battle is touch and go in the air."

"This is true of all armies, jen. We shall manage."

After a few more words the audience was finished and Kapt Logan Lakelmi went off about his duties. Alloran threw a bolt of cloth at Opnar and his helpers, swore at them, told them they must find finer stuffs than this shoddy, and went off to eat his customary huge midday meal. After that he went down in panoply to see about the new arrivals whose ships, having anchored or moored up, were discharging their freight, both human and material.

He was joined on the battlemented walls above the harbor by his nephew, Jen Cedro. The twin suns streamed their magnificence, the air crisped with the tang of openness and the sea and of bracing good health, gulls wheeled and screeched, the breeze blew amicably, and the crowds of folk gathered to watch the new arrivals and speculate upon the treasure brought with them.

The argenters, ships of broad beam and comfortable lines, of plain sail configuration, could hold immense quantities of cargo. Already lines of slaves were shuffling to and fro along the narrow gangplanks, empty-handed outwards and massively burdened on the inward journey. The scent of the sea and the breeze did much to subdue their odors.

The mercenaries came ashore, pretending to lurch about on dry land after their weeks at sea, skylarking, pleased to have arrived safely. Alloran eyed them meanly. Cedro provided the kov with his own telescope, and this Alloran employed to give himself a better idea of the quality of these warriors. He let fall an oath.

"There any many women there—Jikai Vuvushis!"

At the back of the two men, keeping out of the way yet ready instantly to step forward if his advice was sought, Kapt Lakelmi reflected that the Battle Maidens had served the kov well in the past. That view was shared by the entire group of women standing a few paces along the ramparts watching the bright scene spread out below.

All the women's faces turned to the kov, as though a flower-field came alive under the suns.

Standing perfectly still, Lakelmi put his tongue into his cheek so that a bulge jutted above the line of his beard. His lips remained closed. He fancied he was about to enjoy himself.

Chuktar Gilda Failsham, brusque, hard-bitten, her handsome face seasoned by experience, battle, and manipulating men and women, was clearly about to speak her mind. She was a member of the Order of Sisters of the Sword. As a chuktar,

Gilda Failsham was in overall command of all the kov's Warrior Maidens and was a well-trained and competent commander. She did not suffer fools gladly, and suffered men even less, although at times acknowledging that they had their uses.

"My lord kov," she called across the small intervening space along the rampart walk. "There are indeed a goodly number of Jikai Vuvushis. For that we should give thanks to the Invisible Twins—do you not agree?"

Intemperate, hot-headed, consumed with self-pride and arrogant he might be: Kov Vodun was not a fool. He had lost much of that gravitas which had once clothed him in the aura of superiority and integrity so comforting to those he commanded. But he was still a man of substance. He could not manage the fulsome smile the situation might call for; he did say: "You are right, Gilda. Completely so. I am sure you are aware of the esteem in which I hold your girls."

Lakelmi sighed inwardly and took his tongue out of his cheek; he felt disappointed, cheated, even, of a spot of amusement.

Among the small group of women, Lyss the Lone, also sensed disappointment. How satisfying it would be if only Gilda Failsham—who was a splendid if misguided woman—should fall out with this rascally Kov Vodun! Among any collection of people forming a circle or a court around a great noble there were bound to be jealousies, rivalries, secret hatreds and plots hatching thicker than snow on the Mountains of the North. In her experience, which she would be the first to admit was hardly extensive, she had known precious few courts where intrigue did not flourish.

Around the Emperor of Vallia had assembled people who made up what to her represented all that was best in the new Vallia. Even around the Prince Majister intrigue carried on in whispers and furtive glances. This saddened her. Here she was, risking her life with these Opaz-forsaken blots with Alloran, and for all she knew some loose-lipped bastard could blow away her cover and reveal her to the merciless interrogations of Kov Vodun Alloran and his damned sorcerer and their thrice-damned torturers.

Despite the brilliance of the day, the streaming fires of Zim and Genodras, the cooling breeze, she felt choked up, suffocated.

She favored the lord Cedro with a look that should have melted him where he stood.

Neither he nor his uncle the kov had spoken a single word about what had passed in the room where the dead chavonth and their two dead comrades spoke eloquently of great deeds. Not that she worried over that. It merely pointed out what these people were like.

She'd sent little bandy-legged Lon the Knees off very smartly, swearing him to absolute silence about what he had seen. He had been only too tremblingly anxious to agree. She had a meeting with him later. She didn't want the good Lon running off at the mouth. No, by Vox!

The news of that unhanged villain the Kataki Strom beating Drak in a battle was grim and unpleasant. She knew Drak was safe because had he been killed or captured the news would have gone around like wildfire. That was the obvious common-sense reason she knew Drak was unharmed; the real reason she knew was that had Drak chanced on ill she would know at once and with the utmost certainty, know it in her heart.

Standing here with these unpleasant people watching more reinforcements for their benighted army streaming ashore, she sighed. She thought of home. Her life had not so far turned out the way she would have wished. She had hoped that Drak's sister, Lela the Princess Majister, known as Jaezila, would have married her brother, Drayseg, named for the emperor. But that had not happened. Lela was off somewhere in Hamal, enamored of a Prince of Hamal called Tyfar, and the pair of them circling around each other without the least clue how to come to grips with what fate had ordained for them.

As for Drayseg, the last she'd heard of him he was a zhanpaktun somewhere in Balintol. All very distressing. And to cap it all this fat luxurious Queen Lush was openly going after Drak! It was unbearable!

Silda Segutoria, known in these unhealthy parts as Lyss the Lone, returned her attention to where it belonged, as a dutiful little Jikai Vuvushi dancing attendance upon a damned traitorous kov—the bastard.

Chapter Four

In which Lyss the Lone keeps a straight face

The complex series of ceremonies, rituals and religious observances that would transform Vodun Alloran, Kov of Kaldi, into King Vodun of Southwest Vallia, were planned to run for a whole six days. This, said the know-alls, was pitching it just about right. Any less amount of time would indicate faint-heartedness upon the part of the kov, a lack of certainty, even more probably, a lack of the wherewithal. To run longer than a Kregen week would smack of inflated ambition and ego beyond control, which would—inevitably said the wiseacres—bring down the just vengeance of the gods.

A number of dissatisfactions gnawed at Alloran among which he felt most resentment that he was not able to crown a queen. Mercenaries seldom marry in the nature of their employment, unless they settle down to a long-term bodyguard occupation. His plans to marry the Kovneva of

Rahartdrin, and thus lend color to his claims upon the island, had failed to materialize.

He slid his rapier up and down in its scabbard with his left fist wrapped into the fancy hilt. He scowled. The old biddy! Katrin Rashumin, Kovneva of Rahartdrin, had fought his armies from the hedges, from the ditches, had battled from the mountains, and had at the end escaped somewhere across the sea.

All pursuit had failed to discover her.

Well, one day she'd be found, dead or alive. When that day dawned, Alloran would think afresh how best to act. Possession—that was the key! He held Rahartdrin fast in his grip. Soon his armada would sail north for Tezpor.

The other dissatisfaction lay all around him.

He sat slumped back in a huge winged armchair, his feet in gleaming boots stuck arrogantly upon the polished table. Each time he rammed his rapier down, the chape hit the floor. Well, golden chapes would be no problem now, for the island was potentially enormously rich and he'd sweat everyone here, make 'em work. He'd buy or capture more than enough slaves so as to make every kool of the island give forth its wealth.

But—this was Rahartdrin, this town was Rashumsmot. They were not home. They were not Kaldi and Kalden.

And this town wasn't even the proper capital of the island. That was Rahartium, and that place was in a mess. He'd tried to prevent the fires, and then to extinguish them; the task was beyond the powers even of the fabled Nath of legend and song.

He took the conqueror's grain of comfort in the knowledge that to be seen donning the crown in a foreign and defeated country aggrandized him. He could always arrange further coronations to be held in his own provincial capital of Kalden.

When he was emperor, of course, he'd have to be crowned and enthroned in Vondium.

That was all ordained.

He had no doubts about that outcome whatsoever.

Well—he swung his boots off the table and stood up ready to march out to the waiting crowds—well, so far all had gone as prophesied. Arachna* had always been right. In the future his confidence could only increase.

The bedlam of noise of the crowds hit him like a surge of intoxication as he stepped out onto the balcony alone. He waved to the mob. The declining suns showered faces and heads with slanting glories of emerald and ruby, brought blood-red winks of light from the weapons of guards and soldiers, sheened rivulets of viridian down their armor.

Among the crowds and posted at vantage points around the square somberly clad men and women watched all that went forward. At the first sight

*Arachna. Prescot says he has translated this name as Arachna because the original in Kregish was of extraordinary length and complexity and inappropriate for normal terrestrial use.—A.B.A.

of anyone lifting a bow to take a shot at the kov, a far faster trigger finger would contract loosing a crossbow bolt to snuff out the impious idiot's life without compunction.

Waving, managing a grimace that would pass for a smile at the distance of the balcony from the ground, Alloran showed himself to his people. To his new people. Most of the civilian crowds were native to Rahartdrin. His functionaries worked on transferring their allegiance wholeheartedly to him. That was a skill. He used men and women with skills, and used them skilfully after his own fashion.

Nath the Goader had managed to convince his questioners that he had known nothing of the loosened bars of the cages. He was completely innocent. When this was reported to Alloran, the kov had merely said: "The rast's duty was to know all concerning the wild beasts. He failed. He is of no further use."

Then, he'd paused, and a real smile passed over his face. "Yet he can still be of use—in place of handling the beasts he can feed them—with his own body."

His retainers and functionaries showed they appreciated the jest.

Now he waved one last time, and stepped back from the balcony feeling the solid sound from the mobs as being, if not totally, then convincingly genuine.

Using people as he did, Alloran had no use for a failed tool, no compunction in its disposal.

The folk who served him knew this.

When he went to the newly decorated robing room to change his clothes from the ornate and easily distinguished applause clothes to equally magnificent but far more elegant evening wear, his servants made no mistakes.

Clad in gorgeous silks and dripping with jewelry, Kov Vodun strode into the chamber he already called the banqueting hall.

The late owner of this villa still dangled over the town's battlemented walls, and some portions of his anatomy remained intact.

Food and drink in gargantuan quantities was served. The banquet catered for a hundred diners, and of them all only Naghan the Obese and Glenda the Slender ate more than the kov.

Quite a few among that hundred flushed and gluttonous crowd drank more than the kov . . .

Afterwards, replete, Alloran was escorted to his private withdrawing room. He waved away a pearl-draped Sylvie who would have waited upon him, and went in alone. The door was closed on his order: "In one bur!"*

He sat on the divan, kicked off his light slippers, hoisted his legs up and so, putting his head upon a silken pillow, nodded off to sleep. If he dreamed, he had no memory of it when the door opened and a flunkey, nervously, said: "One bur, my lord kov."

He roused himself; servants provided golden bowls filled with warm scented water, and softly

*bur: the Kregan hour, 48 to a day, each of 50 murs. A bur is 40 Earth minutes long.—A.B.A.

fluffy towels. Refreshed, he allowed his slippers to be placed upon his feet. He stood up, adjusted his rapier and dagger belts, golden-linked and gem-encrusted, automatically clicked his rapier up and down, and, satisfied, left the withdrawing room.

Along the corridors guards stood at measured intervals. They wore gaudy costume for fighting men; but they were all well-tested by now and Alloran trusted them as far as any prudent ruler trusts his bodyguards.

Full-fleshed, confident, Alloran strode along and the subservient lackeys followed after, as was proper.

He did not have far to walk before he reached the double doors covered in dark green velvet, studded with golden nails and decorated with a border of engraved golden panels. He'd had that door installed. When he built his own palace he would still arrange a series of chambers beyond a door just such as this that would still not be a long walk away.

Farther along in a cross corridor walled in blue marble stood Battle Maidens on sentry duty. Alloran merely flicked a quick glance at them, before lifting his heavily ringed right hand and knocking three deliberate times upon the golden lockplate. A girl appeared in the blue-marbled corridor looking with a fixity of purpose upon each Jikai Vuvushi. She could smell the distant odors of stale cooking, yet Lyss the Lone did not wrinkle up her nostrils in disgust. In this place and at this time that could be misconstrued, could prove a most expensive mistake.

She moved smartly from one girl to the next, and as she did so she looked down the corridor. Sideways on to her, Kov Vodun was knocking upon that mysterious green door.

Lyss the Lone very much wanted to know what could be beyond that ornate door.

Very much indeed.

If Alloran continued his routine tomorrow, as he had for the past few days, then at this precise time he should be knocking on the door. That was the reason Lyss had taken it upon herself to inspect the girls of the guard at this precise time.

Alloran's current light of love, Chemsi the Fair, lived in a plush apartment in the top floor of the west wing of the villa. Lyss felt confident Alloran did not have a woman behind the green door he visited every evening.

Chuktar Gilda Failsham, despite being a member of the powerful Order of the Sisters of the Sword, kept her light of love, Ortyg the Burly, in vast comfort in the upper rooms of The Blindell and Korf.

All over the town there were plenty of men and women being kept as a light o' love by someone of position and wealth. These were facts of life that had to be accepted as perfectly normal for the times.

She had stopped long enough and must cast a most critical eye over Sosie the Slop, who was always the worst turned-out girl in Lyss's pastang. Although a Jiktar, she commanded merely a company-sized pastang of sixty girls, and Gilda, although a Chuktar, commanded the small three-hundred-sixty-strong guard regiment. This was a perfectly normal arrangement for bodyguards and differed from the regular structures of the line.

"Well, Sosie, and what is it tonight—ah!"

"It came off in my hand, Jik—I swear it!"

"Oh, I believe you, Sosie, I do. You will just have to sew your buttons on much more tightly. Won't you?"

"Yes, Jik."

Turning away, Lyss said, not unkindly; "I'm glad I'm not a man with whom you might fall in love, Sosie. He'd go in dire peril, believe you me."

Swinging back, Lyss stared stony-faced at Sosie. The girl's full lips twitched, a barely perceptible tremor. Then her face became as stony as that of Lyss.

Satisfied, Jiktar Lyss the Lone marched briskly off.

"As Dee Sheon is my witness!" she said to herself, crossly, striding along. "If a task is set to your hands, then that task must be performed as well as you possibly can and with all your heart and mind and muscle. I hate a sloppy regiment. So I drill and train and discipline the girls—and for what? So they can go and fight my friends who serve with Drak! It is really monstrous."

She could see the funny side of it, though . . .

As a Sister of the Rose, she knew she was a member of the very best sorority there was without having to think about it. The Sisters of the

Sword, the Grand Ladies, all the other female Orders, secret, martial, mystical, charitable, it mattered not, paled beside the magnificence that was the Order of the Sisters of the Rose.

Among the regiment commanded by Gilda were a bare handful of girls from the SOR, and none knew Silda Segutoria. She had kept away from the new arrivals, and would take enormous care investigating them, unseen, before introducing herself as Lyss the Lone.

She was off duty in half a bur and would then keep her appointment with Lon the Knees. She would far rather be breaking and entering the rooms behind that infuriating green velvet door with its tawdry golden ornaments.

Reaching the left-hand guardroom reserved for the Jikai Vuvushis, she was met by gusts of laughter, a quantity of horseplay, a ferocious squabble over the ownership of a pair of black tights, and a sweeter scent by far than most of the stinks in the villa. She ducked a thrown hairbrush and sidled past two girls indulging in a little arm-wrestling, and so reached the small cubicle-sized space reserved for the Jiktars.

All this was a nonsense, of course. She didn't mind sharing a guardroom with the girls, who equated with the men called swods in the army, the girls having a variety of colorful names. Because the villa was so small for all the people Kov Alloran crammed into the place everyone had to share. At least, she and the other Jiktars did have a private space, and a personal locker and a peg to hang their duty uniforms.

She shucked off the silly tabard-like garment revealing her black fighting leathers. The tabard was stiff with threaded wire—not gold wire. Kov Vodun was not so enamored of dressing up his bodyguards as to throw gold away like that. Rumor had it that all the colors would change once Alloran crowned himself king. She hung the tabard on the peg and heard the smash and crash of something glasslike and fragile breaking outside. The girls were in riotous mood tonight.

They were a good bunch, really. If only they fought for the Prince Majister, for Drak, instead of his bitter foe!

"Got a man for tonight, then, Lyss?" shouted Jiktar Nandi the Tempestuous, shoving her head into the cubicle.

"No."

"Of course," said Nandi, cheeks aglow, hair falling over her forehead, "I should have known better than to ask. We don't call you Lone for nothing."

"You ready to take over, Nandi?"

"I am. But what's your hurry?"

"No hurry. Nothing special. When you bring my girls in I want to be gone. That's all."

"Rucking 'em again, have you? You'll be one of the first to get a shaft through your back, come a battle."

Nandi was only half-joking. Everyone in the regiment knew the strictness of Lyss's control over her pastang.

Without replying, Lyss sat on the cramped

three-legged stool and took off her villa shoes, started to pull on her tall black boots.

Nandi did not offer to help.

Lyss was too bloody-minded to ask.

In this she recognized that herself, the real person sitting here, Silda Segutoria, was perilously close to being sucked whole into this strict and harsh woman, Lyss the Lone. She thought of herself as Lyss for obvious security reasons. To think of herself as Silda, twin to Valin her brother of whom she had not heard for season after aching season, was to court disaster.

She looked up under her eyelashes, both hands on the straps of her left boot.

"When Sosie the Slop trundles in, she is down for four burs' extra duty in the washroom. I'll tell her Deldar on my way out."

"Washroom? Just as well. If she caught punishment duty in the kitchen she'd crottle* everything she touched."

A thin flicker of a smile touched Lyss's lips. Silda would have laughed out loud in delight.

Nandi took herself off, and Lyss, after a last quick look in the tiny oval mirror and a pat at her hair, followed.

She stamped down to wriggle her boots on comfortably, and gave her weapons belts that familiar hitch that settled them comfortably about the swell of her hips. Never one to let herself be

*crottle: A word describing the effects of burning or charring, of over-cooking food so that it becomes tasteless and generally inedible.—A.B.A.

untidy or in discomfort, Silda, in the shape of Lyss the Lone, followed that maxim to the best of her ability.

She headed directly for the nearest exit of the villa. Many of the massive and ornate statues had been removed merely to provide that amount of extra space. The marble floor looked paler and more polished in squares and star-shapes where the statues had stood for so long. Lyss moved with a sure easy pace, not swinging about too much, keeping in a straight line. People passed, going about their business. She felt a pang at the sight of slaves in their gray breechclouts and kept her face set in that stony mask.

Raised voices, as of a group of people all talking at random, reached her from the hall leading to the exit. She walked on and saw the group entering the building, a gaggle of the new arrivals being led to take up whatever duties they had been assigned. If many more bodies were crammed in here the walls would burst.

She stopped abruptly. She did not swear out loud; but the soft curve of her lips tightened.

To herself, she said: "Oh, damn! Just my luck!"

In the approaching group and laughing up at a tall Bowman of Loh, walked Mandi Volanta. Mandi had been through Lancival at the same time as Silda Segutoria, and it was sure that she would recognize her. Lancival, where the Sisters of the Rose trained their girls in many arts and educated them for life on Kregen, bred a very special kind of person. Silda was immediately aware of the stab of sorrow and then of anger that Mandi Volanta had turned against the majority of her school friends and against the emperor.

There was nothing else to do but swing about and go marching off back the way she had come and by a circuitous route reach the next exit along, which lay past the Corridor of Bones.

She looked neither right nor left and, with her nose stuck arrogantly in the air, strode on past the detail of Chuliks on guard. For all her attitude of haughty superiority, she was aware of the Chuliks' yellow skin, of their green-dyed pigtails, their round black eyes, and most particularly of the upthrust tusks set in the corners of their mouths. They wore good quality armor and bright uniforms, and their weapons were clean and sharp. Born to be mercenaries, Chuliks, and highly prized.

When she reached the outside air the suns were nearly gone.

Crowds meandered about the streets waiting to gawp at the illuminations to be provided by the kov in this night's contribution to the festivities of his coronation, and no doubt hoping that free wine would flow in torrents.

A musky odor hung on the air, compounded of sweat and dust and the exhalations of many people. The streets echoed to the surf roar of the crowds, and the occasional shrill yells of laughter piercing through did not sound incongruous. Lyss hated it all.

All these people should be shouting for Drak and the emperor. Still, she could hardly find it in her heart to blame them too harshly. Those ferocious Chuliks back there and all the other warriors under Kov Vodun's command would quickly smash them back to their new obedience.

Already there were drunks lurching disgustingly about the streets.

Taverns were doing, in the liquid jargon of the profession, a Roaring Trade. Dedicated drinkers were not hanging about waiting for job lots of free wine from the kov that might or might not materialize. The worshipers of the circle around Beng Dikkane, patron saint of all ale drinkers in Paz, were not going to soil their lips with wine, free or not. So the liquid refreshment flowed and, inevitably with people of small brain capacity and inferior character, the drunks staggered about.

With the last upflung rays of red and green scoring the darkening sky the twin suns sank, Zim and Genodras settling down for the night. And, to relieve them on their eternal vigil over the face of Kregen, the fourth moon floated into the evening sky, resplendent with light. She of the Veils shone down in fuzzy pinks and golds, lighting the whole world in her own special and mysterious way.

Silda—off duty she was firmly going to be Silda and not Lyss—always felt comforted when She of the Veils drifted serenely in the night sky. She knew that many of her special friends felt that way, too.

Now the four hulking lads, two sets of twins, whose names were Ob, Dwa, So and Ley Dohirti, must have been imbibing very freely very early. Otherwise not a one of them in his right mind would have offered to insult a Jikai Vuvushi. They each carried a heavy wooden cudgel, as was the right of any free man of Vallia.

With the four clumsy farm lads, and undoubtedly the cause of the trouble, Nath the Sly urged them on. He was short, slightly built, squinted, carried a knife and was a very devil in determining to have his own back on the whole world for not providing him with a powerful fighting man's body that would attract the girls. He was a stylor at the farm, and ink smudges stained behind his ears and along his fingers. He squinted up at Silda, leering.

"A prime one this, lads! Ready for the plucking."

Nath the Sly had heard those words used in a mummer's play only three days ago, the actors prancing in a canvas booth, and he considered them apt to the situation and himself as an educated man for quoting poetry.

"A real right beauty," said Ob Dohirti, and hiccoughed.

His twin, Dwa, spluttered out: "I'll fight you for the first—"

"Plenty there for us all," cut in Nath the Sly, anxious to avoid internecine warfare. "Grab her now!"

Silda did not know if these louts had chosen their spot with cunning skill or if the fortune of Coggog the Unmentionable had blessed them. She did know that as she swiveled to face one pair of twins, her hand going for her rapier hilt, the other pair rushed in from the back.

Used to snaring recalcitrant animals on the farm, the Dohirti twins used a twisted rope with great skill. Silda felt the strands lap about her, tangling her arm.

"Keep her quiet!" yelped Nath the Sly.

The spot in question, either chosen by these five cramphs or by the chance of Coggog's favor, gave the opportunity for the twins to drag Silda into the black mouth of an alley penned between sheer brick walls. Burn marks, like distorted clouds, showed in the moon's light on the brickwork. Windows were boarded up. Silda knew the place all right, for it was a structure selected by Alloran to be demolished to make way for his building extension program.

She kicked and got a black boot into a gut, and then thrashed aside with the other, and missed a vital spot, and then she thought it was time to start screaming.

Nath the Sly took out his knife, held it by the blade, and clouted Silda over the head.

At once she slumped, her body went slack, and she fell all asprawl with the rope into the blackness of the alley.

Chapter Five

Of Lon's Fine Feathers

Silda toppled forward into blackness and slid herself forward over worn cobbles. A single tap from a knife hilt wielded by a scrawny runt like this specimen wasn't going to knock her out. Her head donged a trifle, as though the famous bells of Beng Kishi tolled muffled.

Her onward movement stripped the tangling rope away from her arm.

This situation was very familiar indeed from her years of training at Lancival. There they taught their girls how to take care of themselves.

The men were already arguing fiercely among themselves.

"Grab her, you great hulu!"

"Git outta the way!"

"Can't see a thing—"

"That's my foot!"

A rough hand raked along the cobbles after Silda's boot.

Obligingly, she rolled over onto her back, peering back to see the silhouettes of the men against the vague luminosity of the moon-drenched street. She felt regret, as she lifted her boot, that as a zorca-rider she did not wear spurs. Still, the boots were solid. The heel crunched down with a nice juicy smack.

One of the louts yelled blue bloody murder.

In the next intant Silda was on her feet and the sound of the rapier as it whipped from the scabbard jolted half an ounce of sense back into the drunken heads.

"She ain't—"

"She's got her sword!"

Nath the Sly felt cheated.

"Get on her, you fools!"

One of the men surged forward, a black batlike shape.

Silda had no wish to slay them. Oh, yes, there were plenty of girls who would joy in sticking a length of tempered steel into their bellies, one after the other. But Silda's emotions were held in check. She was a cool fighting machine, and as such not about to spill blood that could be avoided. Her cover remained more important than simple vengeance.

Delicately, she pinked that outstretched arm.

The fellow yelped as though branded and stumbled back.

"Onkers! Idiots!" Silda poised ready for anything.

"Get her!" screeched Nath. He did not lunge

forward, preferring to leave the heavy stuff to his half-drunken companions.

Standing in the darkness she was practically invisible to them, while they stood out as black silhouettes.

"Run off, you unhanged cramphs, or I'll spit you through, one after the other! *Bratch!*"

They did not bratch there and then, although they hung back. Nath whispered ferociously and Silda just glimpsed in time the upraised arm and the flung cudgel.

The common folk of Vallia are adept and swift at throwing cudgels and knives.

She ducked. The wood clipped her across the forehead, bounced, clattered against the cobbles. She felt a wave of dizziness sweep over her, and ground her teeth together and fought the ugly wave of weakness that dragged at her knees. She remained upright, warily watching, and she used her training to push away the pain.

"Right, you rasts. You're done for now. By Vox!" she got out, half-gasping. "I'll have your ears!"

Her head felt light, like a feather, and as she moved forward that silly head seemed to want to go ahead on its own, her body stumbling after. She flicked the rapier into line. The little 'un. He was the bastard to go for . . .

One of the men husked out: "I'm off. Come on—she's probably got no gold, anyway."

Silda lined up, poised, and lunged.

With a cry of pure horror Nath the Sly leaped like a salmon, just avoided the blade that would have skewered his right arm. He took the point in his elbow and for a breathless heartbeat Silda fancied the rapier would hang up entangled in his bones. She whipped it free and immediately slashed it hard down the arm of the next fellow.

That settled it.

Their clumsy farm shoes clattered on cobbles.

This unpleasant incident, Silda was aware, was one of the ugly results of drink.

Except—except that little 'un, the one the others called Nath, had clearly been intent on dark business.

Well, there were thousands of Naths on Kregen, named for the fabled hero of many an epic legend. Nath was just about the most common and most favored name in Kregen. The precious metal Nathium was reputed to hold magical qualities in its silky texture. She put her left hand to her forehead, and felt stickiness.

She had not drawn her main gauche. The whole stupid incident hardly seemed to merit great concern. She took her hand away from her forehead and lightly touched the brown leather and canvas bag slung at her side.

Poor hulus! If she'd. . . . Well, they'd have either run screaming, or tried to scream without faces. . . .

It was absolutely imperative then for her to lean against the greasy wall and to suck in draughts of the evening air. She did not so much shudder as let the shakes cleanse the feeling of dirt from her.

After that, wiping her forehead, she cleaned

the rapier on the oiled rag all prudent warriors carried against this kind of eventuality, and sauntered out onto the street.

There was, of course, no sign of the four drunks and their evil genius, Nath. What his sobriquet might be, Silda did not know. Probably it was the Cunning, or the Clever, or the Fixer.

Plenty of the girls she knew would piously hope that the little runt's elbow would seize up and would never work properly again.

And, being apim, Homo sapiens, he had only two arms.

The various races of Kregen blessed with four arms, or a tail hand, were, she had often thought, extremely lucky. To have four arms in a fight! Or to have a tail with a dagger strapped to the tip, or, like the Pachaks, a hand with which to grasp a blade. . . . How perfectly splendid that would be!

Walking along, she kept herself more on the qui vive than she would have done before the fracas. Lon the Knees had said that he did not think The Leather Bottle would be the nicest place for a lady to meet him, and had suggested an inn, The Silver Lotus, which he considered suitable. In the ordinary course of his life, Lon would never dream of entering so expensive and so—to him—high class an establishment. But he'd mumbled something to her about a deal he could arrange, and she'd gathered he was going to do something particular to find the silver stivers necessary for admittance.

People like Lon, and those louts back there,

habitually worked in copper or bronze coins. Silver was hailed with joy. Gold—wha' that?

Just about the only way they'd get their Diproo-fingers on gold was the way they'd tried in the alley. And, to be sure, during the Times of Troubles many lawless men had snatched more gold than they, their fathers and grandfathers, and sons and grandsons, would ordinarily see in their combined lifetimes.

Lon the Knees, face aflame, nose a purple beacon, eyes brimming, looked splendiferous. He glowed. He waited under the dismounting porch so that he might enter the inn with the lady, and glory in the feeling that all eyes would be fixed upon his companion.

"Lahal, Lon."

"Lahal, my lady."

Silda composed her face. Then she contrived a dazzling smile. She really wanted to bust a gut laughing.

Lon! Lon the Knees! His famous bandy legs were encased in riding breeches that almost fitted, and their color owed more to judiciously applied brown chalk than to natural cloth. He'd borrowed those, that was for sure. Yet they were not too far removed from the usual Vallian buff breeches the gentlefolk wore.

His boots glittered. Silda did not make too close an inspection of them. But that superb polished shine, that had come only from loving ministrations right here under the dismounting porch, for most people's boots were dusty if they walked a pace or two. Her own were a sorry mess compared with Lon's.

And his coat! Now where the hell had he got that from? Originally the garment had been a khiganer, a heavy brown tunic that fastened by a wide flap along the left side of the body and along the left shoulder. The neck came in a variety of styles, and this specimen possessed what appeared to Silda to be the highest, stiffest, most constricting neck she'd ever seen fitted to a khiganer. Lon's chin jutted out like a chick sticking his neck out of the egg.

The arms of the khiganer had been cut off to reveal the loose flowing sleeves of Lon's shirt. The color was ivory, for he did not wear the normal bands of color denoting allegiances. Silda was prepared to take a bet that Lon was wearing sleeves and no shirt at all.

He wore no hat. This was probably, Silda decided, because he had been unable to beg, borrow or steal one of the typical Vallian floppy hats with the brave feathers. His own headgear, a skull cap, a head band, would be quite inappropriate here.

The main gauche was thrust down into his belt and from somewhere he'd cobbled together a quite respectable scabbard for the dagger.

Lon quivered.

"Shall we go in, my lady?"

"By all means, Lon. I am looking forward to a pleasant evening."

"Shall you wish to see the illuminations, my lady?"

He wouldn't normally speak like that. He was trying to suit his language to the importance of the occasion.

She halted.

"Lon—two things. One: speak nicely but normally. Two: Don't keep on my lady all the time. My name is Lyss. Use it when you have to."

Lon swallowed.

"Yes, my la— Yes, Lyss."

So that meant that Silda was back into the persona of Lyss the Lone again. She sighed and went up the steps with Lon into The Silver Lotus. She'd be damned happy when all this present untidiness was over and she could go home and see Drak. That made her think of that awful Queen Lush. The fat scheming bitch! No doubt at this very minute she was fluttering her eyelashes at Drak, and oohing and aahing, and arching her back—the fat cow—and stinking of too much scent and—and—and she was with Drak! It was just about too much.

Still and all, Silda was a Sister of the Rose, and so Silda must be Lyss and soldier on.

The buttons of the khiganer along Lon's left collar bone, fashioned of pewter, had their embossed representation of Beng Debrant almost polished away. The buttons down his left side started out in exactly the same way, the pewter shining nicely. Halfway down, the buttons were made of bone, some with inscribed and worn away pictures, the lower ones plain. Toward the bottom of the tunic the buttons were of wood. Lon kept his right hand casually across his stomach as much as he could, concealing those wooden buttons.

The Sisters of the Rose learning at Lancival were told that if a person made an effort, if they did the very best they could, and tried to their utmost, then, win or lose, they couldn't be faulted. The results of those contests lay with the Invisible Twins made manifest in the light of Opaz.

Lon had made a tremendous effort.

Silda gave him full marks.

She was uncomfortably aware, with a feeling she tried to tell herself was not self-conscious superiority, that in Lon's mind no thought of any sexual approaches existed. He was just pleased to be out, and to be seen out, with a young lady of so different a background from those girls he habitually consorted with. And the very thought made Silda feel conscious of her unworthiness. How her sisters in the SOR would chortle at her now! And—she'd tell 'm all to go hang!

The inn was of the middling quality, clean, and the wine varied from reasonable to good. If some patron felt the rush of blood to his head and ordered a bottle of Jholaix, there was just the chance one might be found. The chance was very slender, for of all the wines of these parts, Jholaix was acknowledged to be the finest. Its cost was astronomical. She turned to Lon as they sat in the seats indicated by the serving girl, and said: "Something very simple, Lon, for me."

He stared at her with a concerned expression.

"Now, my la—Lyss—in the lights, I can see. Your head—there is blood—"

"Oh!" she said crossly. "Didn't I wipe it all off?"

She hauled out the kerchief and spat on it and scrubbed, wondering what the hell her mentors would say if they could see her.

"Each time we meet, Lon, I am bloody. Take heed."

"How? I mean—what—?"

"Louts, drunken, out for a laugh and robbery."

"The Watch is lax, I think." Then Lon let one eyelid droop. "Which is fortunate, at times. . . ."

Silda laughed.

The serving girl was a Fristle, all laypom-colored fur, and a saucy tail, and brushed whiskers, clad in a yellow apron. She was not, therefore, a slave. In her meek obedience Silda sensed much of a slave's mentality.

"I am parched. I would like to start with a glass of parclear. The fizzy sherbert will clear my throat."

"Two," said Lon, importantly. "And, after?"

The Fristle fifi said: "There is quidgling pie, roast chicken, any kind of fish you require, ordel pudding—"

"Ordel pudding for me," said Silda unthinkingly.

"Two," said Lon again.

"Wine?" Silda twiddled her fingers on the table. "As I said, keep it simple."

Lon said, "What would you like?"

Decisively, Silda said, "Kensha, with herbs."

"Two," said Lon.

Was that a slight nervous gesture to the wallet-pouch strapped to his belt? Silda fancied she'd have to be highly tactful if it came to push of pike, as Nath na Kochwold would say.

Kensha wine, a delicate rosé, was best drunk with a sprinkling of herbs into the glass. They gave the wine a lift, a fragrance and turned it from merely a good cheap wine into what was truly a fine vintage.

So the evening progressed, eating, drinking and talking. The usual subjects of conversation were dealt with gravely by Lon. He was seething and bubbling inside with delirious pleasure. He'd live on this night's dinner for the rest of his life in memory, drawing spiritual nourishment when he drank up his cabbage soup and gnawed a heel of cheese or a crust of bread. This girl was superb!

He told her that Nath the Goader had vanished. He, himself, had been exonerated. All the same, he'd sweated blood for just a little too long . . .

When he apologized for his coarseness of expression, Silda laughed out loud, hugely amused. She was enjoying this evening as she'd never imagined she would. The day had been fraught enough, Opaz knew.

The Silver Lotus was doing moderate business, people entering and leaving, and folk nipping in for a quick one before the illuminations. A brilliant laugh from the opposite corner of the alcove drew Silda's attention. A woman was in the act of throwing her head back, laughing with open enjoyment at some sally of her partner's. Her black skin sheened with health, her raven's-wing hair shone like an ebony waterfall, and her eyes gleamed with a challenging brilliance. Her ankle length gown of eye-catching emerald green suited her superbly, and the silver adornments were in perfect taste.

On her left shoulder a little furry likl-likl crouched contentedly munching on the scraps of food she passed up, the little pet no doubt proud of his silver-studded green collar. The silver chain attaching him to the woman's left wrist glinted as she moved.

Her companion's teeth shone in his black face as he laughed with her, gallant in decent Vallian buff, with bright bands of color to indicate his loyalties. They made a dazzling couple. Silda warmed to them. She did not know their names, nor was she ever likely to; yet she sensed this unknown woman was relaxing and letting the evening take over, rejoicing in her good fortune, letting life be lived and flow by.

A noisy party entered, all chaffing the old jokes between themselves, and sat down around a table across from the couple who had so aroused Silda's admiration. The water dropped in the clepsydra, and a serving girl turned the glass over, and Silda began to think that she must now see about the possibly unpleasant business of ending this enjoyable evening.

She had ascertained that Lon the Knees really did know nothing about whose hand had loosed the bars of the wild animals' cages. He genuinely had no idea who might have done that hideous deed. He had not shared whatever macabre fate was reserved for Nath the Goader only because it was proved by subsequent inspection that his bars had not been loosed, that the very size and ferocity of the churmod had splintered them through.

Lon swallowed and lifted the last of the herb-fragrant Kensha in his glass.

"Shall I—that is, Lyss—do you wish to see me again?"

The true answer was that Lon had failed her. She had hoped to pursue the lead afforded by that mysterious hand loosening the bars of the cages. With that as a dead end—why, there was no reason to see Lon again, was there?

He drank the last of the wine down, looking at her. She wetted her lips and realized she could not destroy his happiness so callously.

"Of course, Lon!"

His smile in that florid face would have warmed up the Ice Floes of Sicce. He reached down to his wallet on his belt, and Silda saw his face go stiff.

The smile dwindled. The color fled from his cheeks, and his nose lost its purple sheen, and shriveled.

"Lyss! My money—it is gone!"

Chapter Six

Tavern brawling—Silda style

No doubt whatsoever entered Silda's mind that Lon was lying, was trying to trick her into paying. She had summed up the animal handler, and she trusted her own judgment.

Lon had gone to a tremendous amount of trouble for tonight. He had obtained his wonderful costume from somewhere. He had silver enough in his wallet to pay for what they had consumed. She was convinced of that.

So—some thieving bastard had stolen Lon's money.

Instantly, she said: "Don't fret over paying, Lon. That presents no problem."

"But! My lady! I cannot—"

"I'll have a word with the landlord. Thieves will do the reputation of his establishment no good at all."

"I'd like to—"

"Quite."

Something light touched Silda's side, a feather-like glancing touch she barely appreciated. She opened her mouth to chide Lon and to tell him to brace up, when a shrill agonized shriek burst up from the seat at her side.

She looked down, shocked.

A round furry bundle rolled onto the seat.

She knew what the little animal was, at once. The spinlikl, with a body of multi-colored fur, and eight long prehensile limbs each equipped with a powerful clutching hand, was one of the favorite methods by which the Thieves of Kregen secured their loot. A spinlikl could move about with amazing speed and deftness, quiet as Death, and open locks and bolts, steal treasure, and return to its master or mistress worth a fortune.

She turned sharply as the spinlikl, screaming, gathered itself on seven of its eight limbs.

The eighth limb glistened brightly with blood.

The animal sprang past Silda. Swiveling her head she saw it clambering up to the shoulder and neck of the man who sat at the next table along. His face was that of a hairy Brokelsh, uncouth yet powerful, and now that lowering visage was black with anger.

"What have you done to my lovely Lord Hofchin?" the Brokelsh bellowed. He grabbed the flailing arm and blood spurted. "You have fairly cut his hand off!" And, indeed, the poor creature's hand dangled limply with the blood pouring out.

Silda knew what the poor creature had done. After he had stolen Lon's money, he'd opened her brown canvas sack and groped inside with that hand that was now half lopped off. Served him right, of course, yet he was not to blame. His master, who trained him in all the arts of thievery, was the true culprit.

Two other hairy Brokelsh sat with the thief. Now they stood up, hands going to their belts where weapons dangled. They were all decently dressed in finery that chimed well with the festivities, bright colors, and sashes, feathers and the wink of imitation gems.

Lon stumbled up onto his feet, passionate with rage.

"You rasts! You stole my money! I'll have you—"

He started around the table and Silda snapped, sharply and impatiently: "Lon! Sit down!"

"But—"

The thief snarled his words, quite as angry as Lon. "Have me, hey? I'll have your hide!"

One of his companions stared down the dining room. "By Diproo the Nimble-fingered, Branka! Keep it down. Here comes the landlord. . . ."

This Branka, white-faced and savage at the damage to his spinlikl Lord Hofchin, would have none of it. He ripped out his clanxer and started for the table where Silda and Lon still sat.

Silda stood up.

"Landlord!" she called in a voice accustomed to ordering regiments about. "This rast has stolen our money. I intend to have it back off him. You may send for the Watch if you wish."

With that, Silda Segutoria, the daughter of Seg

Segutorio, started for the thieves. She drew her rapier.

"Lyss!" Alarmed, Lon dragged himself up, lugging out the main gauche.

This thief, hight Branka, sneered at the rapier. "That pinprick, missy? I'll show you what real tavern brawling is all about!"

'Like this?" said Silda, and snatched up in her left hand the chair and hurled it full in the fellow's face. Her left arm, hard and muscled from long hours with the Jikvar, powered the chair so that it smashed the fellow's nose, knocked out an eye, and sent him tumbling backwards into his companions.

She didn't stop there.

The screams from the staggering men meant nothing. She snicked the blade through the arm of one of them, withdrew, slashed it across the guts of the next so that his fancy clothes all fell down, and then she was on Branka.

He was shrieking and gobbling on blood. Half his teeth were knocked down his gullet. His eye dangled. His nose spouted blood everywhere.

Silda ignored all that, carefully making sure she did not touch the mess. The spinlikl crouched on the floor, whimpering, sucking his damaged limb.

Silda dived her own fist into Branka's wallet and dragged out a handful of coins.

"Lon!"

He was just standing there, goggle-eyed.

"Yes, Lyss—"

"How much?"

He swallowed. "Uh—seven sinvers. Oh, and four obs."

Again Silda did not doubt Lon's honesty. If he said seven silver sinvers and four copper obs, that was what had been stolen. She sorted the money out and started to put the rest back, then she paused.

"The rest of this is stolen, too, I suppose. Landlord!"

He was standing there with his hands wrapped in his yellow apron and his eyeballs out on stalks.

"Yes, my lady. I am here. The blood—"

"You've seen plenty of that before. Keep the money and let the Watch sort it out. You have a nice place here, but I wouldn't let your clientele know that you allow this kind of thief free access."

"But, my lady—"

"We are leaving now. Tell the Watch. Oh, and what is the reckoning?"

"No, no, my lady," he babbled. "Please, say no more. You have been troubled in The Silver Lotus. I am desolated, please, my lady, with my compliments. . . ."

"That is considerate, under the circumstances. Here, your money, Lon."

Lon wasn't sure if the money could ever make up for the glory of the moment. What a girl this Lyss was!

As they went out, Silda noticed the black couple staring after them eager and alive and thoroughly enjoying the free entertainment.

The lady stroked the furry likl-likl crouched on her shoulder, and the creature's bright eyes regarded with great wisdom the fracas upon the floor and the maimed form of the spinlikl. They were not related much as species, although, obviously, they shared much physiology in common. Also, Silda was reminded there were other reasons for carrying a likl-likl upon the shoulder.

Yes, they were lovely little furry bundles, to be stroked and cuddled and petted, splendid companions. They were friendly little creatures, only resorting to violence if aroused by some extraordinary cruelty. The spinlikl had made no attempt to steal from the black lady in the emerald green dress. Her likl-likl would have known at once and set up an outcry.

The other fact that had not passed unnoticed by Silda was Lon's possession of silver in the form of sinvers, the currency of Hyrklana, among that of other nations. The stiver was the usual Vallian silver coin. This meant, clearly, that the new recruits from Pandahem had already been parted from some of their cash. There'd be dhems as well, silver coins of Pandahem, circulating. Well, as they said on Kregen, gold and onkers are like oil and water.

The ugly side of this was that nations over the seas were sending men and money to assist this rast Alloran in his dreams of conquest.

Outside, as they walked along the street heading for the Urnhart Boulevard, the illuminations were just beginning, brightening the sky. She of the Veils rode behind a wisp of clouds, gilding them with her light.

Lon wasn't concerned with the illuminations.

Oh, no, not when he could walk along with this superb girl at his side and be, as he was confident they were, the cynosure of all eyes.

"Well, Lon," said Silda in her fine free way, striding out, lithe and limber, "a free night's dinner can't be bad, can it?"

"By Beng Debrant, no!"

They strolled on, savoring the air, seeing the sky erratic with the illuminations. People hurried past.

"Fish hooks, was it?" said Lon.

"Fish hooks? Ah—er, yes, that's it."

"Just because I borrowed the belt and wallet from one-eyed Garndaf, I didn't have my own, which is nicely defended with fish hooks. The spinlikl is known to defeat the hooks, though. Well-trained animals can."

"So I have heard."

"Yet, yet—Lyss—the thing's hand was nearly off!"

"It looked worse than it was."

"Yes, but—"

"The Watch must have marched up to The Silver Lotus from the other direction, for we have not passed them. I trust they were in time."

"Clumsy, those Brokelsh. Nature has not cut them out to be thieves. Not like Crafty Kando."

"Crafty Kando?" A zephyr of impending delight passed across Silda's mind.

"Why, yes, Lyss. He's the most cunning disciple of Diproo the Nimble-fingered I know. And I've known some in my time, I can tell you. Why, back when I was in the army there was—"

"Yes, yes, Lon. But this Crafty Kando. You know him well? He is trustworthy in a thief? Can I meet him?"

"Why, Lyss!" Lon was shocked.

"Don't be so po-faced, Lon! Can I meet your friend, Crafty Kando? I may have business with him."

"You won't give him to the Watch? That's not—"

"No, no, that's not it. There is something I must do, and I have been racking my brains to find a way to do it. Now, by Vox, you may have found the way!"

Chapter Seven

Secrets around the campfire

This time the battle was more prolonged, swaying to and fro, and finally ending in stalemate. Drak could feel the ache in his bones, the tiredness dragging him down. He could always remember in those longago days when he was a child his father saying: "Tiredness is a sin, my lad. Brassud! Brace up! If you use your willpower and your spirit you can always find the extra strength to go on."

It was damned hard. But it was true. As a Krozair of Zy Drak had learned the Mystic Way. He could control himself. He was well aware of the way people regarded him.

The upright one, they'd say, dedicated, solemn, filled with niceties and integrities, never willing to admit to defeat. He supposed this was true. As for himself, all he ever wanted was a happy life with his father and mother, at home in Valka. Oh, yes, he loved Delphond, and Desalia, his mother's estates along with the Blue Mountains. He'd not had a lavish private province of his own, only Vellendur, of which he was Amak; but it was a tiny island for when he was emperor he would come into all the imperial provinces.

He could envision life there doing all the things he liked to do. And here he was, acting as the Captain of a Host, running a war, and not doing very well at it, either.

This fight, which no doubt the scribes would call the Battle of Cowdenholm, ending in a draw, saw both armies haul off and make camp. The fires painted the clouds in lurid oranges and reds. There were no billets or barracks, and it was bivouacs for those lucky enough to find something with which to build them. Drak, Prince Majister of Vallia, sat hunched in his cold cloak before the fire, and felt sick.

The First and Second Kerchuris of the First Phalanx, and the Fifth Kerchuri of the Third Phalanx had done splendidly, as ever. Their massed array of pikes had broken the wild leem-like charges of the foe and hurled them back. The heavy infantry, known as churgurs, had fought like leems themselves. The cavalry had foamed across the field like tidal waves. Yes, all in all everyone had done splendidly; but it had not been enough.

Reinforcements had come in from Vondium, notably those madmen of his father's bodyguards. Everyone had fought to the limits of their strength. And they had not broken the enemy forces commanded, as he now knew, by this evil cramph,

Strom Rosil Yasi of Morcray. He was a damned Kataki, one of that low-browed and violent race of diffs who were slavemasters under any circumstances. The Kataki Strom's twin brother, Stromich Ranjal Yasi, was not here. No doubt he was somewhere else stirring up trouble and enslaving innocent people.

He stirred himself as Jiktar Endru Vintang walked up to the fire, shivering and holding his hands out to the blaze.

"The prisoners, jis," began Endru.

"Yes, yes. We took that traitor Chuktar Unstabi, I believe. His damned archers caused us some grief before you charged them."

Endru was far too politic to remind the Prince Majister that when Vodun Alloran was being sent down to the southwest to regain his province, it had been Drak himself who hired on the Undurker archers. And this had been against the wishes of the emperor.

"There are also some Katakis taken—"

"Hang 'em all."

"Oh, yes, never fear, jis."

"If there's one thing the country folk like to see it's a damned Kataki swinging in the breeze by his neck."

"And Chuktar Unstabi?"

About to order the same summary justice, Drak paused.

"Send him to me under guard. I will question him."

"Quidang!"

"We have not taken anyone of so high a rank as a Chuktar in this war. He might sing."

Everyone knew that Drak, like his father, would not tolerate torture as a means of gaining information.

When Chuktar Unstabi wheeled up with a detail of Endru's men, grim-faced, about him, Drak felt the sorrow.

He glanced up, seeing the wreck of the archer's uniform, the wound in his shoulder, the hangdog look of him.

"When last we met, Unstabi, you swore allegiance to me and I hired you on. You went with Alloran to the southwest, and you turned traitor. Tell me why you should not be hanged."

Unstabi was not bound. He fingered the golden pakzhan at his throat.

"What can I say, majister? Hang me, and have done."

The man's long-nosed face, canine, held nothing of the usual supercilious look of an Undurker. He hailed from the Undurkor Islands, a group off southwest Segesthes, west of Balintol. He had sailed a long long way to find his death. But then, was not that the fate of many and many a fine paktun?

"By Vox!" snapped Drak. "You mean that?"

"Yes. I am not a Pachak who gives his nikobi, his gift of honor, and so foolishly fights to the death to earn his hire. I am a zhanpaktun. But, majister, I cannot explain why I left your service so willingly and fought for Kov Vodun Alloran."

"The emperor warned us of the dangers of

mercenaries, and will not hire paktuns. He was right, at least in your case. What d'you mean, you can't explain?"

The long canine face turned, as it must have turned many times in battle to loose the Undurkor arrows.

"Just that when the kov said he would take control, make himself king of south west Vallia, and then Emperor of Vallia, it was the most natural—"

"Emperor of Vallia? Is the rast bereft of his senses?"

"I think so, majister. Also, I think sorcery—"

"Ah!"

Endru felt the chill. His men remained fast about the prisoner; but Endru knew they, too, did not relish the way this conversation was going.

"Well, Unstabi. Tell me."

Somewhere off in the night hard-faced men were hanging Katakis and rejoicing that the opportunity had come their way. Chuktar Unstabi probably knew that, too. He said, "May I beg a sip of water, majister?"

Crossly, Drak said, "Oh, give the Chuktar a mug of wine. Have you eaten, Unstabi?"

"No, majister. But if I am to die—"

"Sit down, you fambly, and eat something. I want to know all you know of this damned sorcery Alloran has. By the Blade of Kurin! Cold steel is one thing. But wizardry. . . ."

"Aye, majister," said Unstabi, unsteadily sitting down. "That is indeed foulness from the Pit of Untlarken."

Drak didn't agree entirely with that, not that he knew what the Pit of Untlarken might be, although it sounded unpleasant. His good friends and comrades, Khe-Hi-Bjanching and dear old Deb-Lu-Quienyin, were Wizards of Loh. They were the most famed and feared wizards in this part of Kregen called Paz. Now they were off somewhere on their own mysterious errands. But they did weave a net of thaumaturgy to protect the family of the emperor. That, Drak knew, was a fact.

Food on a wooden dish was brought and although it was cold and congealed, Unstabi wolfed it down, and then swigged back a jug of wine. He wiped those canine lips.

"All I know, majister, and I give you thanks for the food and drink, is that Kov Vodun vowed vengeance on those who had ruined his province of Kaldi, one day. The next, he was friendly with the two Katakis, and was planning his career as king and emperor."

"Katakis are not renowned as sorcerers."

"Exactly so, majister."

"Well, then?"

"It is said that Katakis, seeing only slaves in the world for their use, make good tools for those who lust after power."

"That is so, as Vallia knows to her cost."

"The kov once spoke to me of Arachna."

"Arachna?"

"Aye, majister. What that might be I do not know."

"Well, what did he say?"

"That he needed a fine strong man from the prisoners we had taken. Arachna, he said, was most demanding. Also, he said that the helpers were called Mantissae. I gathered they were slaves."

"Slaves and Katakis go together, to the shame of the world."

"Aye."

"And that is all you know?"

Tiredly, the Undurker nodded his head.

"If it has served to keep me alive for another bur, and give me food and drink, then it has served me, at least. But, majister, it is true, as I am a zhanpaktun."

Drak hunched his cloak about him.

"And I suppose, Chuktar Unstabi, you imagine I am going to offer you fresh employment with me? As a hyrpaktun you can hire on as and when you please. Is that it?"

"I had hoped so, majister. But after—"

"Precisely!"

"I can at least, plead sorcery led me astray. And I can offer you information about the Kataki Strom's forces."

Upright, filled with honor, a man of integrity, Drak the Prince Majister might be. He was also not a fool. This kind of information could be invaluable. He saw he would have to bargain for it. And, too, he knew that once he had given his word, Unstabi would know he would not break it.

"Very well." He made up his mind at once.

"You have my word. Your information proving of value, you will not dance on air."

"Your word as a prince of Vallia?"

"Yes."

The canine face allowed at last some expression of satisfaction.

"When Kov Vodun set off to reclaim his province, the emperor gave him the Army of the Southwest. Apart from slingers and archers and churgurs, that army contained the Eighth Kerchuri of the Fourth Phalanx, and the Ninth Kerchuri of the Fifth Phalanx."

This was so. The Eighth and Ninth Kerchuris had straggled back to Vondium. Subsequently, the Ninth had been broken up to replace losses elsewhere.

"Go on."

"They refused to join Kov Vodun. The other regiments of the Vallian army, likewise, refused to join, except a single regiment of slingers. They allied themselves to the body of the paktuns who went over to Alloran."

"I see. What caused that?"

"The sorcery I spoke of, majister. But what I am saying is the kov was wroth at the loss of the phalanx. Such a body is unknown. To me, an experienced fighting man, it has been a revelation. So the kov sought to create his own phalanx."

Drak sat back. Someone brought more wood for the fire. Sparks blazed up like fireflies.

"That takes great skill."

A Phalanx was an intricately built-up structure. Many months of training were needed to persuade that structure to perform as a single giant organism. A static Phalanx was of only partial use.

Any body of pikemen in the field could be called a phalanx; a Phalanx was a particular number of men arranged in a particular way.

The basic building block was the Relianch, consisting of 144 pikemen, called brumbytes, and 24 Hakkodin, the men armed with halberds, axes and two-handed swords. Six Relianches formed a Jodhri. Six Jodhris formed a Kerchuri. The Kerchuri was the wing of a Phalanx, one half, so that the total number of brumbytes was 10368 and the Hakkodin 1738. Also in the Phalanx were lads who ran with caltrops and cheveaux de frise. The missile component consisted of two Lanchans of 432 bowmen forming a Chodku, attached to the Kerchuri.

"Yes, majister," said Unstabi. "Very great skill so to combine all the arms of the phalanx, the pikes and shields, the archers, to make the men obey the call of bugle and drum and whistle. But Kov Vodun suborned—and now I may use that word freely—enough men of the Vallian Phalanx Force to train up his own version of a phalanx."

A low rumble of anger traveled around the tight circle of men who had gathered as the prince questioned the prisoner. Kapt Enwood ground his sword into the mud. Two or three Chuktars showed their displeasure. Jiktar Naghan swore fiercely. Even Chuktar Leone Starhammer said a few words to express her horror. All knew the seriousness of this calamitous news.

Drak summed it up.

"So be it, then. If Opaz wills. One must accept the needle. No man or woman born of Opaz knows all the secrets of Imrien." He heaved himself to his feet.

Unstabi scrambled quickly up as was proper.

"You promised to tell me of the composition of the Kataki Strom's forces, Unstabi, well knowing we must have a shrewd idea ourselves. Yet I encouraged you to speak."

Unstabi stood still. "You are known as a stern and sober prince, majister. Also, as one able to salt a leem's tail. I knew you would understand my information would go further. The bargain is good, majister?"

"Yes, Unstabi. But I cannot hire you on again, as you must see. Give all the facts and figures you can to my stylors. Then you will be provided with a mount and gold enough to see you home to the Undurkor Islands."

Unstabi bowed.

"I give you my thanks, majister. But I am a zhanpaktun and cannot go home quite yet. I accept your gifts and will travel somewhere where they need fighting men."

"So be it."

Not all the men and women gathered at the fire might grasp the significance of the lower case or upper case for the initial letter of the word phalanx; all understood the seriousness of this intelligence. Capital letters are strange beasts in the Kregish, and a slight inflection in the way the word is pronounced can indicate capitals, although in general Kregans are not too fussed over capital letters. What fussed Drak now was that Unstabi had religiously referred to Alloran's forces as a phalanx, not a Phalanx.

This could mean, at a simple level, that some component of a proper Phalanx had not been represented in the men who had deserted to Alloran.

He could remember his mother's telling him once that the word phalanx was not really Kregish, that his father had invented it out of the air, or out of space, from somewhere. The lower case phalanx sounded with an "f." The upper case Phalanx sounded with a "v." This had seemed to him perfectly proper, as it should be in an empire run on sensible lines.

The Vallian Valanx sounded supremely apt.

What the hell this bastard Kov Vodun Alloran was going to do about being crowned king and going on a rampage of conquest among the western islands remained a mystery.

Unstabi, sensing he was dismissed, turned to depart, and then swung back. He hesitated.

"We shall," said Kerchurivax Mantig ti Fillan, "wish to know exact details, Chuktar. So far you speak, as I believe, with veiled words."

Hearing this, Drak checked himself. Mantig was a shrewd fellow. Had Unstabi been fooling the prince?

"I swear—" began Unstabi.

"It may be," interrupted Drak, "that the Chuktar is not aware of the knowledge he possesses. After all, he has, as he acknowledges himself, no real comprehension of the Phalanx. If you question him, Kervax Mantig, I feel confident he will tell you a great deal of what you wish to know."

Mantig nodded at once. "My pleasure, jis."

Of the Kerchurivaxes commanding his three Kerchuris, Drak had, by reason of wounds, sickness, death or promotions, contrived to lose eight of them. That was a high loss rate. In these battles, commanders could fall just like the swods in the ranks. Chuktars Nath the Murais and Larghos the Oivon had been provisionally promoted from brigadiers to divisional generals. Drak valued his soldiers, both men and women, and felt the pangs of agony when they died. No. Far better, for all his stern devotion to duty and his desire to rid Vallia of the reiving human predators leaching her life blood away, far better to be at home in Valka, playing music, reading the ancient books, riding in zorca races, practicing the artistry of the sword, and dancing and singing the night away in the good old Vallian tradition. Far better, by Zair!

So Kervax Mantig ti Fillan, as a new commander of his Kerchuri, was anxious to create a good impression. He would find out the truth concerning that rast Alloran's newly created phalanx.

Chuktar Unstabi tilted his long canine nose a trifle higher into the night air now. The relief in him must be enormous, and Drak felt genuine pleasure that there had been no need to hang him as high as the damned Katakis.

"Yes, majister," said the Undurker. "I will answer every question to the best of my ability."

Drak's thoughts, when he dwelled on a sensible life in Valka or Delphond, did not encompass a vision of a woman at his side sharing that life. Queen Lushfymi was a remarkable woman, there could be no doubt of that. She had played a useful part at the very end of his adventure down in Faol when he'd rescued Melow and Kardo, his comrades who were Manhounds. Mother and son, jiklo and jikla, they were. He would value their presence now. He could remember that return to Vondium when all the city danced and sang, and he'd been swept up into the arms of his mother, the Empress Delia. That had been a homecoming! And—his father, the emperor? That man had been nowhere to be found, he'd just upped and disappeared as he so often did, without explanation.

He had no proof, he just felt with odds of nine-to-one certainty, that his father and mother did not share the general view of Queen Lushfymi. Everyone regarded her with respect and awe, dazzled by her beauty and power, her charm of manner, her jewels and clothes, and more than a trifle apprehensive of her sorcerous powers. Yes, it was quite clear she would make a splendid wife. Her country of Lome, in the northwest of the island of Pandahem south of the island empire of Vallia, might be small. It was awash with wealth even after the wars. Yes, she would be a fine match.

She had not, as a certain other young lady had

done, thrust her body between him and certain death. She had not fought with her life for his. But, then, she was a queen, not a savagely ferocious female Jikai Vuvushi, a sister of the Order of Sisters of the Rose. She hired other people to fight for her.

Still Unstabi waited on his dismissal now that the conversation had again included the Prince Majister.

Kapt Enwood, bluffly, was saying to the three Kerchurivaxes that he'd want more information from the Undurker zhanpaktun than only intelligence on that rast Alloran's new phalanx.

"We'll have him, aye, and his rascally Kataki Strom. We have more reinforcements coming in. We'll have that Kataki by the short and curlies, and hang him higher than any of the whiptails we've hanged today, by Vox!"

"Amen," said Leone Starhammer.

Drak roused himself.

"After today's standoff," he said, and he put force and dynamism into his words. If he was supposed to be the leader, he'd damn well lead, by Zair! "Today has shown us that we will win. Strom Rosil Yasi must know his strength will dwindle as ours increases. A few days to rest the troops and put fresh heart into them, the reinforcement sent from Vondium joining us—and we shall sweep the Kataki Strom away!"

Growls of savage agreement rolled throatily around that group of people clustered about the Prince Majister of Vallia.

And then Chuktar Unstabi, the Undurker mercenary, said: "It will not work out like that, majister. If you gain any significant victories here and threaten his own province of Kaldi, the kov will gather all his forces from the islands and hurl them against you on the mainland." He stared about the group. "I thought you realized that."

Chapter Eight

With the Jikai Vuvushis

The two ladies, stripped stark naked and with bodies heavily oiled so that the mingled lights streaming from the high windows ran liquid runnels over their skin, sized each other up and then grappled with savage ferocity.

"Hai Hikai!" screeched Chuktar Gilda Failsham, and hurled herself on Silda, grasping hands cunningly reaching for holds on that smooth slippery body.

Both ladies had their hair bound up tightly. They gripped fast, chest to chest, squirming to change grips and so throw the other onto the matting floor. That coarsely woven matting might be softer than the hard boards beneath; a heavy fall and a sliding slip across it could scorch up skin woefully. Silda was not prepared to let that happen to her so she slid Gilda's first impetuous attack. She twisted the heavier woman over and instead of depositing her upon the mat held her long enough so that she could flail out an arm and seize Silda by the upper leg. Silda rocked aside and Gilda, a hoarse cry of triumph bursting unstoppably from her, crashed down—underneath.

Silda allowed the Chuktar to do the obvious next step and roll over. The matting stuck to her bottom; but it was nowise as nasty an experience as falling upon it with that portion of her anatomy. She took a professional's pride in thus allowing the Chuktar to win. She felt it politic to win the odd fall or two—and then she'd let poor Gilda Failsham drop down to feel what it was like—but as for emerging the victor in these bouts, why that, she'd decided, might not be clever in a spy.

Gasping and panting, heaving herself up, rosy and oily, Failsham blatted out: "You are improving, Lyss; but you have a long long way to go in the art before you best me."

"Too true, by Vox," said Silda, and stood up in a single fluid motion that would have knocked out the eyes of any mere male spectator. Here, in the private villa given over to the Jikai Vuvushis, any man venturing in might not return with all he brought with him.

The girls sitting on the benches arranged around the salle laughed and cheered. Silda was not convinced that not one of them had the skill to penetrate her deception; probably Mandi Volanta could. She'd chosen her time, pounced, catching Mandi as she was toweling her hair, and said in her most winning and at the same time most compelling voice: "It were better, Mandi, if we pretended not to know each other, and most particularly to keep secret that we are Sisters of the Rose. Do you agree?"

"I am shattered, Silda! You—here—why, I—"

"My name is Lyss the Lone. You do not know me."

"As to that—by Dee Sheon, you gave me a start!" The towel slid down Mandi's neck. Then, recovering herself, for she was, after all, one of the SOR, she went on: "Of course I agree we know nothing of the Rose. But—why should we not acknowledge that we know each other?"

"It is best. Do you agree?"

"Oh, yes, if you wish it, Lyss," said Mandi, crossly. Silda did not heave a sigh of relief. She was well aware that the intolerant yet basically kind and sound training of Lancival produced people perfectly capable of handling this essentially simple circumstance.

"Although," and here Mandi looked studiously away from Silda. "I own I am most surprised to see you in the service of Kov Vodun. Why—I thought you were devoted to the emperor and that iceblock of a son."

Silda took the proffered opportunity.

"I thought he was not an ice block."

"Well, he must be with that Queen Lush for all one hears. A dreadful family, all told, don't you agree?"

"Oh, quite dreadful."

So Silda was gratefully aware that one problem was neatly overcome by the process of Mandi's quick wits and native cattiness constructing the theory that Prince Drak, the Prince Majister, had turned his face away from Silda Segutoria. She had, then, Mandi's theory went, taken herself off fuming with anger and frustration and bitterness, and joined up with Kov Vodun. Out of spite.

After a few more cautionary words, Silda added: "Oh, and, Mandi, by Dee Sheon, it is good to see a familiar friendly face here."

"Is that why they call you Lyss the Lone?"

"Life sometimes presses down with the weight of all the marble in Pentellharmon's Quarries."

Mandi looked meaningfully at Silda's brown canvas and leather bag hanging at her side.

"I see you carry your—"

"The bag passes muster as an ordinary knapsack that any soldier might have. It contains other items, as well."

"I shall do the same. But, do you use—?"

"Only when forced. We in Vallia know of the Sisters of the Rose, and I sometimes think folk begin to know too much."

"They will never know, not while the mistress lives."

"That is so."

With that problem if not out of the way then temporarily shelved, Silda could concentrate on her upcoming meeting with Crafty Kando. Lon the Knees, when they next met was full of apologies.

"He is not to be found, Lyss. I have searched out all his usual haunts—ahy, and I had to stick a weasel of a fellow who tried to rob me. But Crafty Kando has gone to ground."

"I will try to be patient, Lon."

She could guess that Lon was rather pleased. The delay meant he had the excuse to see her again. She had summed up Lon as a man who would not lie too much to gain his ends with her; with those for whom he had contempt, for the slavers whom the poor folk slanged as greeshes, he would pile lie upon lie and joy in it.

So, perforce, Silda had to wait in patience, and drill and discipline her pastang of girls, and stand guard duty, and ride out with the kov on his journeys. He was now King Vodun—at least in his and his cronies' eyes—and she would have to get used to addressing him thus. It stung.

When the girls sitting around the walls on their hard benches cheered Chuktar Gilda Failsham on yet another victory, Silda carefully avoided looking at Mandi Volanta. Flushed, rosy, shining with oils, the women passed through the warmed corridor to the Baths of the Nine. There they wallowed in luxurious steam, hot, warm and ice cold water, and so emerged at the end, spruce, glowing, filled with vigour and ready for what the world of Kregen might bring.

"Mind you, Lyss," said Gilda Failsham in a reflective tone of voice as they walked toward the refectory. "As the kov—the king—keeps us as his personal palace bodyguard and we have not seen a proper fight for a long time, we cannot expect to receive too many of the new girls into the regiment."

"They are to form a new regiment, I believe."

"Yes. By Kurina's Steel! Some look likely. But there are far too many I would not trust on the field at my side, let alone at my back."

Thankfully, Silda knew that would not occur for her. She could not face the prospect of actually having to go into a battle and fight against Drak and his soldiers. She'd just up sticks and desert and return to her proper allegiance. She would have failed in her task if that happened; but the thought of fighting against her own friends disgusted her.

"We are to have a few of the new girls, Lyss. And we can send some of ours in replacement." Failsham slid a sidelong look at Silda as they sat at the scrubbed wooden tables and the slaves scurried with food. "I suppose you will send Sosie the Slop into the new regiment. You are to have five more girls to add to your pastang."

This was an eminently sensible arrangement. Any commander would dismiss her worst soldiers, get rid of them to some other unfortunate. The best girls would be taken into Alloran's own private regiment of Jikai Vuvushis.

The delicious aroma of vosk pie wafted to Silda's nostrils. Momolams, yellow and succulent with butter, piled on the side dishes. There were vegetables in abundance. She indicated to the serving wenches what she required, and as her plate filled, she said: "Well, Gilda, no. I would like to keep Sosie. Oh, yes, she is a Slop. She is a mess. But she fights well."

"I cannot pretend to be surprised. Just make

sure the king never catches her looking like the wet end of a mop."

Silda smiled, and went on: "I would like to claim one of the new girls for my pastang. Mandi Volanta. She looks useful."

Jiktar Nandi the Tempestuous leaned across the table and waved her knife in Silda's face.

"You have sharp eyes, Lyss. But I will not claim her, for her name and mine—well, confusion is to be avoided in a fight."

"If you cannot remember or disentangle names," said Chuktar Gilda Failsham with prim smugness, "you will soon find yourself cut down and shipped off to the Ice Floes of Sicce."

"Oh, yes, of course!"

"As to this Mandi Volanta, Lyss. Yes, you may take her into your pastang."

"Thank you, Gilda."

Nandi used that dangerous knife to spear a chunk of vosk pie. "She and you, Lyss, are of the Sisters of Renunciation. A strict Order, I hear. I do not see why you don't join us in the Sisters of the Sword."

The name Sisters of Renunciation was often used by members of the Sisters of the Rose as a cover name. It was a well concealed secret. Now Silda smiled again and chewed her vosk and cabbage without replying.

The deception was not quite meaningless, for the vast majority of the SOR had not gone over to Alloran. They had remained loyal to the empire and the empress. And, that meant they were loyal to the emperor as well. Once a Sister of the

Rose went into action as only a girl of the SOR could, why, then, there would be no concealing the secret from anyone who understood. She felt that even had Lon the Knees seen the fight with the chavonth clearly, he still wouldn't really have grasped what he was looking at.

There was no doubt about it, in the special and particular Disciplines of the SOR, Silda Segutoria was quick, was extremely quick, was a most rapid lady. . . .

The brown bag called a knapsack she wore might not be as easy to open and close as a more normal jikvarpam, which besides being designed for the job with specially strengthened corners and sides and a fastening that would not delay nimble fingers by a hairsbreadth, would have a few rows of bright red stitching to distinguish it from the next girl's; but the knapsack looked just as it was supposed to look. Any girl was entitled to a bag to carry her kit in, surely? No one was going to think for an instant the humble canvas bag was a jikvarpam, were they now?

Silda sincerely hoped not.

The refectory began to fill as the officers of the regiment drifted in, sniffing the food, licking their lips at the odors of wines.

". . . kicked him where it made his eyes water," said one of the Jiktars, casually, sitting down and reaching for the wine, evidently finishing a story.

One of her Hikdars, sitting at her side, laughed and said: "Apt, Jik."

The Hikdar on the other side said, "Of course,

Jik, if you go on like this you'll cause a calamitous population drop—"

"A what drop?"

So they all three laughed.

Bright conversations, laughter, the clink of cutlery and glass, the rich odors of first class foods and wines, the taste of luxury all about, all these sensations crowded in and they made Silda Segutoria hopping mad. Confoundedly angry! These stupid women all enjoying themselves and living high off the vosk were avowedly out to destroy what was left of the responsible and caring part of the structure of management for Vallia. They were going to install a creature like Vodun Alloran. It was outrageous.

Nandi the Tempestuous, gesturing widely, knocked over her glass of wine. She swore and laughed, and flung a taunt at Silda.

"You're looking down-in-the-mouth, Lyss! Drink a little wine—"

"I was just thinking that we are underemployed here."

Now she'd opened the ball, as it were, she'd go on.

"Yes, Lyss?" put in Chuktar Gilda Failsham. She spoke in that tone of voice that brought a waiting silence around the refectory table.

"Why yes, Gilda. Badly so. By Vox! All we do is stand sentry go along the corridors."

A nodding of heads confirmed her words.

The Chuktar said: "We are paid by and in the service of the kov—the king—and obey orders."

"That may be so," objected Nandi, speaking

only just in time as she swallowed a chunk of juicy fruit. "But what about the king's apartments beyond the green door?"

"Yes, yes," called a number of the women. "We are excluded from duty there." "The king keeps us at arm's length." And: "He reduces our status as a guard regiment."

"This may be so." Gilda Failsham frowned. "But the king employs his own Katakis and Chuliks within his most private apartments. That is his privilege."

"By Janette of the Cunning Dagger!" burst out Nandi the Tempestuous. "I'd like to know what goes on in those secret rooms!"

Gilda Failsham shook her head. "I think not, Nandi. It is sorcery, surely. It must be, thaumaturgy, necromancy, witchcraft. We're much better off having nothing to do with sorcerers, as any right-minded person knows."

Chapter Nine

Arachna

Chuktar Gilda Failsham was perfectly correct.

The ordinary folk of Kregen steered well clear of sorcery of any order higher than the corner mage who might find a strayed animal, or cure warts, or make up a potion to entice a negligent loved one.

There were many and various cults and societies and orders of wizards upon Kregen, having different powers. Many a wandering wizard was a fake, gaining his living from the credulous. Everyone knew there were real wizards and witches, people who could shrivel the marrow in your bones.

In the series of confusing chambers and apartments in the private portion of the rambling old villa appropriated by Alloran the Chuliks stood guard. Their small round eyes surveyed what went on dispassionately; when they fought and killed they did so with extreme efficiency. Even renowned fighting men like Chuliks, though, looked askance when a sorcerer walked past.

The figure swathed all in a dark green cloak with the devices of Kaldi upon its breast had a golden chain girdled around its waist from which swung sword and dagger. The figure's arms were folded upon its breast, hands thrust deeply into capacious sleeves. The enveloping hood allowed no glimpse of the face and only a fugitive gleam of an eye told that a mortal head existed within the hood.

The Chulik sentries, sweating of oily yellow skin, martial and chunky in harness of armor, smothered in weapons, breathed easier when the ominous figure in the green robe had passed by. They would furtively rub a thick thumb along a tusk, polishing it up, taking racial comfort from the action.

The eyes within the hood observed these actions; the agile and cunning brain behind the eyes noted, and sighed, and once again returned to devising ways and means of staying alive in King Vodun's palace villa.

For times had changed for San Fraipur.

Never had he been one for shriveling a person's eyeballs out, or melting the jelly in their bones, or turning them into little green lizards. People might believe he could do these things, and that was no bad thing, and if they did believe and he mumbled a few words and wriggled his fingers in the air, then they might feel symptoms that would prove salutary. But as for little green frogs—no, San Fraipur had no illusions about his power there.

He liked to be called San, the title given to a dominie or master or sage. He'd worked hard enough, Opaz knew, up in the island of Fruningen to gain the arcana to enable him to earn his living as a Wizard of Fruningen. He'd served Vodun Alloran faithfully since his father had been killed in the Times of Troubles, seeking refuge with the kov in the mountains as the mercenaries and the flutsmen sought to destroy them. He'd gone to Vondium and been impressed with the proud city even in her ruined state. All his arts and all his skill had been given to Vodun Alloran.

And this—Fraipur was not quite sure what to call the Opaz-forsaken thing—had subverted everything good, had turned the kov, had made him into this quasi-monster of legend, had even caused him to turn his face away from the divine radiance of Opaz.

Arachna. That was the thing's name. Fraipur had sensed the aura there, had shriveled within himself at the evil he felt, and knew it was evil because it stood blackly against the radiance of Opaz. Arachna, and her servants were the Mantissae.

Arachna was the name by which she was known; but still San Fraipur did not know what she was, of what race she might be.

When he thought of her that agile brain of his pained him.

He did know, with very great certainty, that he stood in mortal terror of her and her assistants.

Beside that continuing horror this summons from the kov who must now be called king meant—almost—nothing. Alloran wanted to see him. That, in itself, made this day different from very many that had been blown with the wind.

These interior corridors were never as busy as those outside the green door. Slaves hurried everywhere, of course; but they were a normal part of life. Fraipur did not incline his head as stupid fat old Naghan the Chains the chamberlain passed with his fancy woman on his arm. Fraipur knew little of women. They had been denied to him in his youth during training and he'd never bothered to open new relationships when all the worlds of thaumaturgy lay awaiting his inspection.

Naghan the Chains trembled so that his chins shook; the woman on his right arm looked quickly away, and made a secret sign. Tosie the Hiffim and Naghan the Chains both devoutly believed in San Fraipur, despite the kov's—the king's—apparent recent slighting of the Wizard of Fruningen.

For Fraipur the fact that Naghan and Tosie were walking together like this meant the chamberlain was off duty and was going out. Stupid and fat he might be, but he oversaw protocol at audiences. Anxiety grew in Fraipur like an ulcer.

As he walked through the various sentry-guarded rooms and passageways he saw the changes made since his last visit. This villa was large; but it was overcrowded in the outer parts where everyone was jammed up together and that was largely caused by the amount of space given over to these secret inner areas. The name of the villa had been banned from everyone's lips by the king, and he was in the process of choosing a new name. He did not wish to give the place a too resounding name, for obvious reasons. He also did not wish to give it a mean-sounding name, for equally valid reasons.

At a green velvet door with golden strigicaws decorating the panels, Fraipur halted. The two Chuliks looked at him, and one used the butt of his spear to hit one of the slaves crouched by the door. The two slaves jumped up and opened the double-doors. Fraipur walked through.

In the old days Alloran, like everyone else, used slaves. He had used them with some consideration. Fraipur had not bothered his head overmuch about the new emperor's edict that slavery was to be abolished. He could quite see that the slaves here would welcome that law.

In the anteroom beyond the door he was met by Jiktar Rakkan, who was a Kataki. Fraipur, like any honest citizen, detested Katakis. Now, he kept his face expressionless and followed the Kataki Jiktar, walking as though he trod on eggs.

The next archway, swathed by cloth of gold curtains and guarded by four Katakis, gave ingress to the chamber where Alloran sat in his throne waiting for the wizard.

"Come in, San Fraipur! Advance!"

"Majister," said Fraipur, and he went into the full incline, nose on the carpet and bottom in the air. He was never one to take unnecessary chances. Alloran showed his pleasure at this slavish display, ordered Fraipur up, and waved a slave forward with a stool. The three-legged wooden stool was provided with a green and red cushion, and Fraipur understood this to be a mark of distinction.

He sat down, thankful to get off his knees, which resembled jellies.

"Majister?"

"You have not served me well lately, San. I forgive you in this, as a mark of my pleasure. Now I am king. That washes away all that is past. Now we look to the future."

"Yes, majister."

"I shall test your powers, San. Tell me what I wish to know, and great rewards shall be yours."

"Majister?"

"Strom Rosil Yasi, the Kataki Strom, does not fare as well as he might upon the mainland. You see I am well-served by the Katakis." He waved a beringed hand around the chamber and Fraipur saw the guards along the walls, harsh in black and green, feathers still in the hothouse atmosphere. Low-browed are Katakis, snaggle-toothed, owing little to humanity. Each has a long flexible whiptail to which is strapped six inches of bladed steel. A whiptail can slip that deadly dagger up between his legs and into your guts in a twinkling.

Fraipur swallowed. "So I see, majister."

"Strom Rosil sends news that he needs more men. He has recently been held by that brat, the Prince Majister, and has conducted a strategic withdrawal across Venavito into Ovvend." Alloran lifted a hand and a Sylvie wearing pearls and tissue placed a golden cup of wine into the outstretched paw. Sylvies are so voluptuous that they appear as though dreamlike, capable of gratifying all the hothouse desires of men. Fraipur did not look at the slave girl as Alloran continued: "You know, San, what province lies to the west of Ovvend."

"Your own Kaldi."

"Quite."

"The question then, is one of the relative powers and strengths of Strom Rosil and the Prince Majister, of the numbers of troops to be sent, if any should be sent, and of the chances of success or failure—"

"There will be no failure."

"Naturally, majister."

"Can you tell me, San Fraipur, what is going to happen? And, then, what I must do?"

"As to the first, majister, I will try. As to the second, the king will decide."

Fraipur sat a little straighter on the stool. Yes, he was just deciding in a congratulatory way, that was a most cunning and crafty answer, when the king frowned and leaned forward spilling the wine onto the carpet.

"I *shall* decide, Fraipur! But you will tell me the issues on which to base my decision! By Vox! Must I always deal with imbeciles."

Fraipur shrank on the little three-legged stool. He could feel the hardness of the wood through the cushion.

From nowhere slave girls appeared like ghosts to swab up the spilled wine and to pour more.

The tinkle of their ankle bells affected Fraipur oddly, as though the Bells of Beng Kishi, instead of ringing in his skull, came clamoring in from the far distance. He opened his mouth, not quite sure what to say, when King Vodun spoke with the snap of command.

"Clear out, Fraipur. Return in four burs, and then tell me true. Dernun?"*

"Majister!" yelped Fraipur, and scuttled off the stool and out the golden-swathed doorway, trembling.

The sound of those eternally damned ankle bells followed him, mockingly.

Alloran swigged the wine back and threw the cup casually over his shoulder where a slave girl—a Fristle fifi—caught it expertly.

"Sorcerers!" he said. "And to think I once doted on that man and all he told me."

A figure cloaked all in deep blue velvet, silver trimmed, glided toward Alloran's throne from a narrow side opening. The hood extended in a cup shape to enclose the vast mass of dull black hair, springy as wire. Alloran stood up as the blue-cloaked figure halted before him.

"Is all prepared?"

"All is prepared."

With great satisfaction, Alloran took up a fresh goblet of wine and with this in his hand followed the blue-cloaked figure through the side opening into a passageway. The room at the end of the

*Dernun: an impolite way of saying: "Do you understand?" Savvy? Capisch?—A.B.A.

passage although fitted out as a bedroom, with a broad canopied bed in the center, and dressing tables and mirrors and stools, conveyed the impression of the sanctuary in the inmost recesses of a temple. The walls were draped with blue velvet. The ceiling's blue velvet hangings depended from five central points toward the cornices to create the impression of a blue star. Silver glitter heightened other impressions, and the waft of hidden fans blew pungent scents upon the air.

If this place could be likened to a sanctuary, then the bed represented the high altar.

In the near right-hand corner stood a tall chair facing the bed. Alloran walked steadily to the chair and sat down, resting the wine goblet on his knee. The five other blue-cloaked figures all gave him a slight perfunctory nod of the head, whereat he lifted his goblet to them. He was well aware of the power of these Mantissae. Their wiry hair frizzed into bowls of blackness, their lowering foreheads and snaggle teeth, the ferocity of their natural expressions, gave little clue to the fact they were all female. Their whiptails were curled up into their cloaks; Alloran knew that even here and engaged in these holy rites they would still have six-inches of bladed steel strapped to their whiptails. . . .

When Arachna entered the chamber she formed, as it were, the centerpiece of a small but imposing procession.

The figure of Arachna was entirely covered by a swath of blue silk cloak with a mask drawn across the opening of the hood so that only the two eyeslits gave humanity to that impression of power. Alloran shifted on his chair. Humanity? Well, he trusted so. . . .

The little procession included half-naked boys waving fans, two more of the blue-cloaked Mantissae, a giant and stupid Womox bearing a massive double-headed axe over a shoulder, and a Fristle fifi holding the silver leads of a couple of baby werstings. The bundles of black and white behaved with a docility amazing in spirited puppies.

Arachna was assisted onto the bed by her retainers who then took up positions which did not obstruct Alloran's view.

One of the Mantissae struck a silver gong.

At once another door concealed by the blue hangings opened and a second procession entered.

Fascinated by these slow and deliberate proceedings, Alloran took a sip of his wine. His throat was dry. He looked at the figure of Arachna on its back on the bed, and saw only the two eyeslits. Was she looking at him? What could she be thinking? He dragged his own gaze away to stare at the man selected for this day's investigations.

He stood between four of the Mantissae, naked, his wrists bound at his back. He was a Khibil, with a proud foxy face, with reddish whiskers that now were not brushed up arrogantly but drooped in dejection. A supercilious, superior race of diffs, Khibils, and this pleased Alloran, for the best results could only come from the best material.

A thread of red wine dribbled down the Khibil's chin.

Arachna's voice rustled like bats' wings.

"You have your question ready to ask at the right time, Vodun?"

"I have, Arachna."

"Do you continue to deny Opaz?"

"I do."

"Do you continue in steadfast loyalty to Takar?"

"I do."

"Are you content that Arachna and her Mantissae serve you so well?"

"I am."

With a single sweeping movement as of a bird opening its wings Arachna threw the cloak wide.

On the bed lay a Khibil girl. Artful strings of jewels enhanced her beauty and the lushness of her body glowed into the overheated air.

The Khibil jumped, staggered, was caught and held upright. He could see nothing else in all of Kregen but the most beautiful and desirable girl in that terrible and beautiful world.

"Your question, Vodun!"

Rapidly yet carefully, Alloran asked of Arachna what he had demanded of Fraipur.

Groaning, spitting, fighting with his bonds, the Khibil struggled to break free.

One of the Mantissae slashed his bonds loose.

Instantly, without hesitation, he flung himself forward.

Alloran knew that had the girl on the bed been

apim he would himself have been demonically impelled forward by passions bursting into flame all over his body. The Khibil had been given to drink, and had no control over himself of any sort.

Watching with a fascination that grew on him each time he witnessed this sacrifice, Alloran saw the climax approaching. A Mantissa moved to the side of the bed. She carried a heavy-hilted dagger. The blade was not a Vallian dagger, being snake-curved; Alloran blinked involuntarily, and took another sip of wine.

From under the figures on the bed a hand showed, a left hand. It moved between their legs with deliberate speed down the bed. The hand opened at the end of a long and flexible tail, stringily muscled, ridged, glinting in a shade far removed from the reddish skin tint of the Khibils' bodies.

Into that tail hand the Mantissa placed the snake-curved dagger.

Alloran sucked in his breath and the wine slopped from the goblet.

The tail hand struck. Viciously it sliced the dagger upwards, upwards and in, deeply in. The Khibil's scream compounded of agony and ecstasy shrieked into that blue-draped room. He collapsed. With a gesture finicky yet savage, Arachna pushed him off and he fell limply to the carpet. The Mantissae did not move. No one moved. Blood smothered the breast of the Khibil girl.

The voice from Arachna was entirely different

from that with which she had spoken to Alloran. It husked as though reaching in past cobweb veils of mystery and distance, remote yet penetrating, the voice past reason.

"Strom Rosil will continue to retreat. His powers are limited and grow weaker. You must seize the leem by the throat, not by the tail. Water will not always wash away blood."

The voice swelled so that undercurrents of passion shook the husky words.

"You must choose to drink water or drink blood!"

The voice ceased.

Arachna lay still, eyes closed, the blood shining upon the glorious Khibil body. The Mantissae closed in and wrapped the blue silk cloak about her, drew the concealing mask across those glowing features.

Slowly, Alloran stood up. He was shaking with the passions of the sacrificial ceremony.

He was King Vodun of Southwest Vallia! That could not be denied. There was no more to be discovered here and he walked purposefully to the exit. If Strom Rosil failed him. . .

Water or Blood? Would he drink Water or Blood?

Which was more fitting for a king?

Chapter Ten

At the Leather Bottle

Lon the Knees said: "If you insist, Lyss . . ."

"I do damn-well insist, so that's an end to it."

"The Leather Bottle is not the place for—"

"Look, Lon. A poor weak defenseless girl has been known to stick a knife into a hulking great brute of a man insulting her. Well, is that not true?"

"Aye, aye. But—"

"That's an end, Lon! *Queyd arn tung*!"*

They were standing in a shadowed doorway of a respectable street, the Lane of Sweetmeats, and the evening drew on in long mingled shadows of emerald and ruby. Already the Maiden with the Many Smiles floated over the rooftops of Rashumsmot casting down her fuzzy pink light to blend oddly with the last trailing remnants of the radiance from Zim and Genodras. The air

*Queyd arn tung: no more need be said.—A.B.A.

tanged with spicy odors. Folk moved with purpose, to reach home after the day's labors, to find the first wet of the evening, to see what pickings there might be in any of the thieves' quarters abounding in any town where an army is quartered.

Lon stared at this glorious girl, and shook his head.

She wore a beigey yellowish dress that gave a dusty impression and the patterns of green leaves threaded in the material did not please Lon in an obscure way he couldn't fathom. The dress was halfway thigh length and her legs were bare. She wore sandals tied up with, on the left foot, a leather thong and on the right foot a piece of string. She carried her brown leather and canvas knapsack on her left hip.

Over her right hip a frippery of the dress created a flounce that effectively concealed the long Vallian dagger scabbarded to her belt there. Her hair, lustrous and sweetly clean, was tightly bound up. As a Battle Lady she did not habitually let her hair grow long; but she was too much a woman to allow it to be cropped mercilessly, as so many of the Jikai Vuvushis did. Her face, though was not sweetly clean. That gorgeous face was decidedly grubby.

Black spots dotted it here and there, her eyes were smudged, and an unwholesome looking sore extended down from the right corner of her mouth. She'd painted that on herself in this quiet doorway, with her back to the Lane of Sweetmeats and with Lon standing vacantly at her back.

In one of her belt pouches reposed a small vial of a secretion from the skunk-like animal called a powcy. It really did, as one of her dear friends would say, pong 'orrible. So far she had not had the courage actually to daub the nauseating gunk over herself.

If the going got too rough, though, she would—by Vox, she'd stink the place out!

Lon tried one last time.

"Look, Lyss. Yes, all right, we'll go to The Leather Bottle. But if you wore your black leathers and carried swords—"

"D'you think anyone in there would trust me, talk to me? I'd be more likely to be stuck through than I am now, dressed like this."

"Women!" said Lon to himself. "By Black Chunguj! There's no way past them."

With which piece of sage internal logic he set off with Lyss the Lone toward their rendezvous at The Leather Bottle.

As for Lon the Knees himself, his finery had had to be returned from whence it came, that is, back to those from whom he'd borrowed the attire. He wore his own decent rough homespun, a tunic that was improbably hard wearing and might even see him out. The color was indeterminate but tended to the brown. The main gauche was stuffed down inside in its scabbard. He carried a cudgel. He was a Vallian citizen, not a koter, out for the evening and dressed for the occasion.

At that, he'd never really got on with those

danged breeches. Yes, so all right, his legs were on the—curvy—side. But there was nothing like a clean breechclout and bare legs. He felt limber as he walked along beside Lyss, reveling in this aspect of the evening alone.

Even had there not been mineral oil in abundance, folk tended these days not to be so strictly bound by the twin suns in their going to bed and rising. The seven moons of Kregen among them, at different times, cast down light. The Leather Bottle, therefore at this early hour, had not yet begun to hum.

The place looked snug under its low ceil, with wooden benches aptly situated in nooks and with a rotund barrel-row mounted on trestles behind the bar. The landlord polished up a tankard with his upper hands while his middle pair poured drinks for the two Fristles leaning against the bar. They were giving inconspicuous glances to the six Rapas sitting in the bay window, making a deal of noise and clearly intending that this should be the start of a night to remember.

The Rapas looked out of place here, even to Lyss, for no one else was a soldier in uniform, while these Rapas were churgurs, sword and shield soldiers out of one of the new king's regiments of foot. Their feathers bristled, brick red and dusty black, and their fierce beaked faces showed animation as they toasted one another in turn. They were in undress, wearing the king's colors of maroon and gray with the badge of the sea barynth.

"And, Lon," said Lyss when they were served

at a small table in the opposite corner, "you wanted me to come here all dressed up in black leathers."

"Upvil, the landlord, may be an Och, but he knows how to respect a lady." Lon gave her a mean look. "You do not, Lyss, look a lady right now."

"I suppose not." For this night's adventure, Silda Segutoria had consciously forced herself to think and act as Lyss the Lone. So she did not throw her head back and roar appreciation of the neatness of Lon's remark. She just quaffed her ale and looked about, and her right hand rested easily at her side, not too far from her dagger.

The Rapas were kicking up a din so that Lon shook his head and said: "Pretty soon Upvil will have to call the heavy squad and have them chucked out."

"But if they weren't soldiers?"

"Oh, well, that'd be different."

"Well, I hope your friend Crafty Kando turns up before the fight starts."

Lon started to say something, halted himself, and then spat out: "So do I."

His cudgel propped against his stool would be adequate in the typical tavern brawl; against the straight cut and thrust pallixters of the Rapas it would soon prove lacking.

The tavern began to fill, ale flowed, fruits and biscuits were available, and pretty soon customers began to ask for wine. Lon kept on looking at the door. Crafty Kando might be too crafty for his own good in this business, for while Lon did not know what Lyss wanted the thief for, he felt instinctively that there would be profit in it.

There were girls circulating in the tavern, gauzily dressed, clashing bangles, heavily made up and wafting scents that cloyed in the odors of ale and wine and food. They drew shouts of approval and the occasional coin. They indulged in a few ferocious hair and bodice-pulling fights over the money. And still Crafty Kando did not put in an appearance.

Seeing girls in this condition upset Silda far more than watching them on the battlefield.

The people patronizing Upvil's Leather Bottle were mostly from the rough side of life, folk like Lon who did the unpleasant jobs. The regular patrons grew restive with the high spirits and uproar from the Rapa soldiery.

It made not the slightest difference who started the fight. That there would be a fight was perfectly clear. Lon suddenly half-rose and then sank back on his stool. In a low voice he said, "Thank Opaz the Merciful! Here he is now."

Looking quickly toward the door past the bulky shoulders of a Brokelsh just standing up with a bottle in his hand, Lyss saw the fellow in the doorway. He was dressed inconspicuously in drab browns, with a down-drawn hat obscuring much of his features save for a sharp chin. On his hip rested a goodly sized canvas bag.

Then the Brokelsh threw the bottle, the Rapas bristled up with feathers flying, and the tavern erupted.

Lon sprang up to run to the door after Crafty

Kando and was instantly engulfed in a crashing moil of men striking out with joyous abandon. One Rapa was already down with a bent beak. The hairy Brokelsh who'd thrown the bottle ducked just too late to avoid the stool that thwacked solidly into his thick Brokelsh skull. Men were staggering about locked together, others were swinging wild punches, others were flailing with bottles and stools. No one—so far—had drawn a steel weapon, edged and pointed. This was a tavern brawl with unwritten laws.

How long before the Rapa churgurs, massively outnumbered, would draw their swords was in the jovial hands of Beng Brorgal, the patron saint of tavern brawlers.

A big fellow with a purple nose rose up before Lon and hit him over the head with a bottle. Lon yelped, managing to duck most of the force, and stuck the end of his cudgel into the fellow's ribs. He yelped in turn.

A man with the effluvium of the fish market upon him lashed out with his boot at Lon's undefended back.

The boot did not quite reach Lon because a sandal tied up with string stuck itself out sideways and the man's shin smacked into the edge of the sandal-clad foot. The shin came off worst from that encounter.

Lyss didn't stop. Her foot whipped down, planted itself firmly on the tavern floor and her other sandal, with the leather thong, swirled up as she swiveled forward. Her toe investigated most forcefully portions of the man's anatomy that could not bear the scrutiny.

He let out a gargling screech and fell down.

Lyss put her fist into a fellow's mouth and felt teeth break.

She skipped quickly sideways to allow one of the Rapas to go charging past. She let him go and clipped the man following him alongside the ear. The Rapas might be Rapas, fierce vulturine diffs, they were soldiers and they were outnumbered.

The tavern resembled a chicken coop when the fox breaks in. Men—and some of the women—were tangled up everywhere, lashing out, kicking, biting, scratching. Bottles flew. Upvil the Och landlord put his head down behind his bar and wondered if being a landlord was worth the trouble. The Watch might be along soon; by the time they arrived he'd be well out of pocket.

The original locus of the fight around the Rapas had long been forgotten. Men hit anybody handy. It would not have been surprising if one Rapa had hit another in the confusion.

Lon dragged himself off the floor, whooped a breath, spotted Lyss hitting a Gon beside his ear, and yelled.

"He's run off!"

"Well, run after him!"

Lon's face empurpled to match his nose. He dragged in another breath smelling the dust of the floor mingled with spilled wine and blood, and thought savagely to himself what he wouldn't yell out at Lyss.

"Run—in this lot! Like flies in treacle!"

He climbed up onto his feet and instantly a bulky fellow tangling with two furry Fristles collided with him. He was knocked flying again, skidding across the floor on squashed juicy gregarians, the fruit greasing his swift passage under a table. That fell over on him and the tankards of ale upon it liberally baptised him with libations to Beng Dikkane the patron saint of all the ale drinkers of Paz.

Lon shook with frustrated anger.

He clambered up, his cudgel still gripped in his fist.

His hair fell over his eyes. He glared about. There was red in the eyes of Lon the Knees.

He spotted a Rapa and a Brokelsh, representatives of the diffs who'd started the fracas, locked together, each trying to throttle the other.

Lon marched over, knocking a fellow out of his way.

He used the cudgel twice.

One blow knocked the Brokelsh senseless to the floor.

The other struck the Rapa down so that he collapsed in a flurry of his own feathers.

Someone grabbed Lon's arm.

He swiveled, enraged, swinging the cudgel up for a blow that would brain this new rast troubling him.

Lyss said acidly, "We didn't come here to enjoy ourselves! Your friend's run off and he'll be long gone if we don't—"

"Oh," snapped Lon, swinging the cudgel away

from Lyss's head. "He'll be in some sewer by now. Forget him for tonight."

Lyss breathed hard through her nose.

"I suppose you are right. By the foul armpit and lice-ridden hair of Sister Melga the Harpy Herself! This is another day wasted."

Lon was taken aback by her vehemence.

The fight caterwauled on, the noise prodigious, the maids all run off, the air thick with flying stools and bottles.

"Well, Lyss. I suppose we could try The Dancing Flea."

She fixed the animal-handler with an eye of gimlet steel.

"Let us do that."

They moved aside to let a man somersault between them and go thump onto his head on the floor.

"Is there no back way out?" Lyss jerked her head at the doorway. "That's choked up worse than the first bend in a zorca race."

"Yes. Through the kitchens."

"Lead on."

A couple of times Silda had heard the emperor add a word that sounded like "makduff" when he'd said that.

Duff was one of the many Kregish names for spoon, for each size and use had its own nomenclature, and what a black spoon had to do with leading on Silda couldn't fathom. One of these fine days she'd ask the emperor. If Opaz smiled, that was, and she wasn't shipped off to meet the grey ones on the Ice Floes of Sicce . . .

They whistled through the kitchens without stopping. Upvil's charming Och wife, wringing her hands in her apron, watched them wide-eyed. The serving maids huddled, although some of them were peeking through the half-open door taking a lively interest in the entertainment. The smells of the kitchen faded as Lyss stepped out into the night air.

"This way," said Lon, and started off at a brisk trot.

In the fuzzy pink moonlight they hurried along, watchful, naturally, as any sensible person must be in a town of Kregen where soldiers are quartered and there is counter-deviltry afoot. Not everyone accepted Vodun Alloran as the new kov instead of Katrin Rashumin as the kovneva, let alone as some new puffed-up king.

Lyss the Lone, thinking as Silda Segutoria, intended to make more stringent inquiries concerning this aspect of the new regime in Rahartdrin.

The distance was not far and Lon led her into a side street, the Alley of Washerwomen, where he halted at the front of a tumble-down building. The place next door no longer existed, having been demolished in the battle, and on the other side an even more disreputable construction loomed blackly with no discernible purpose.

"This it?"

"Aye. This is The Dancing Flea."

Lyss wrinkled up her nose.

"Yes, Lyss, well. You are sure?"

"Let's not have all that again, my wild churmod trainer!"

He had to smile at this, and pushed the door open.

By comparison, The Leather Bottle was a veritable top-class establishment. The clientele looked as though they'd far prefer to slit your throat than stand you a drink. Shifty faces, furtive eyes, unshaven chins, hands hovering above weapon hilts—oh, yes, a Sister of the Rose would understand hell holes like this.

Silda had often felt that any self-respecting man would either grow a proper beard or shave himself clean. Two or three days' fuzz on the chin gave a man a dirty look. He couldn't be bothered, he was on the down trail, a trail no doubt littered with empty bottles. Some men, she'd been told with sneering laughter by some of the girls, actually thought they looked romantic unshaven. When they scrubbed that bristle brush down a girl's cheek when they embraced her, surely they didn't think she enjoyed the experience?

Moustaches, of course, were an entirely different and exciting matter . . .

Lon's quick birdlike gaze took in the familiar scene, spotting quondam friends, people he might rely on in trouble, allies, and also those he would not turn his back on, those indifferent to his welfare, and those who were deadly enemies. Of these latter he could see only one, black-browed Ortyg the Kaktu. He was sitting with his cronies playing the Game of Moons at a side table.

There was no sign of Crafty Kando.

Lon said, "You'd better wait outside, Lyss. I'll ask Ob-eye Mantig if he's seen Kando."

Before Lyss could reply, a girl wearing light draperies and imitation gems, her face plastered with paint, her hair a frizz of blonde in which the tiara-like vimshu glittered artificially, glided up and threw a tankard's contents in Lyss's face.

Lyss licked the suds off her lips and wiped a finger across her eyes. The stuff was very thin beer.

Lon yelped: "Climi! You crazy shishi!"

"We don't want her in here!" Climi swung the pot back. "Clear off!" She threw the tankard.

Lyss stuck up her right hand, took the tankard out of the air and hurled it back. The pewter edge struck Climi on the forehead. For an instant she stood. Then her eyes crossed and she slumped down, her gauzy tawdriness swirling like the canvas of an argenter being handled.

Instantly, with a bull roar, Ortyg the Kaktu reared up. The Game of Moons went flying. He ripped out a knife and charged headlong for Lon.

"Run, Lyss!" yelped Lon.

Silda Segutoria battled with the persona of Lyss the Lone. One said: "Run, you fambly!" The other said: "Run from that scum?"

By that time it was too late.

Ortyg threw himself at Lon. The animal-handler used to fractious beasts twisted aside and swung his cudgel. Ortyg was quick and the blow missed. He roared back, foaming.

Lon ducked and Lyss put one fist into Ortyg's guts, kicked him in the face as he doubled up and smashed a hard edge down on the back of his neck. Only then did Silda take over, grab Lon and fairly bundle the pair of them out through the door.

They ran up the Alley of Washerwomen.

At the corner they halted and looked back. There was no pursuit.

"He wasn't there, anyway, Lyss."

"No. As I said, another day wasted. Next time you get hold of Crafty Kando, Lon, we'll meet in a place where we don't get into a fight the minute we draw breath!"

Chapter Eleven

Drak changes plans

The black-beaked yellow-winged flyer soared on through the early morning mists, tinted palest apple-green and soft rose-red by the veiled radiance from Zim and Genodras. The breeze blew past the flyer astride the flutduin's back; but no blazonry of apparel in fluttering scarves and trailing cords, no swirling confusion of feathers, marked the flutduin or his rider out from the half-squadron who flew escort right, left, above and below and to the rear.

Drak, Prince Majister of Vallia, flew this early morning recce patrol in person. His brown Vallian eyes looked down past the curve of his mount's neck. His brain noted, numbered and catalogued all he saw.

The bird's powerful wingbeats carried him on in a long undulating series of perfectly judged strokes. Drak did not have the opportunity to fly a flutduin as often as he would have wished.

There was, truly, little to compare with the experience. Riding a zorca, well, that was superb in its own way, a quite different way from this joyous flight through thin air.

Two ulms* off and spread out below like toy soldiers on parade lay the host of Rosil Yasi, Strom of Morcray; Kataki.

Despite the nibbling advances made and local victories gained over him, the Kataki Strom still could field a formidable force. Drak's icy brain went on figuring the numbers, the formations, the qualities and types of the troops spread out below.

The Jiktar who had taken command of this half squadron to escort the prince shrilled a warning cry. He used his long flexible lance to point up and ahead.

Well, by Vox, you couldn't expect to carry out a recce without meeting opposition.

Strom Rosil's aerial component consisted mainly of fluttrells and mirvols, birds and flying animals in general use among the aerial cavalry of many nations. So far as Drak was aware, the flutduin, which he considered the best of all saddle birds, was to be found only in the country of Djanduin. His father, who was the king of that distant land down south in Havilfar, had organized the supply of top-quality flutduins to his island stromnate of Valka, to the east of Vallia's main island.

*ulm: five sixths of a mile, approximately 1,500 yards. A dwabur equals five miles.—A.B.A.

A goodly force of flutduin aerial cavalry had been built up over the seasons, and a fresh colony had been established in his mother's province of the Blue Mountains. The more hidebound elements of Vallia had resisted this uncanny idea of fighting from the backs of great birds of the air; but the proof of the soundness of the scheme had been seen when the aerial cavalry of Hamal, among other nations, had so plagued Vallia.

Drak would have liked a force of Djangs from Djanduin. Those four-armed warrior Dwadjangs were among the most formidable, powerful and feared fighting men of all Paz.

Still, the Valkan flyers he had with him, trained up by Djangs, were efficient at handling their mounts in the air and consummate in the art of aerial combat.

So he had no real problems over the patrol that flew down toward his own little force. The recce was almost over, in any case, and he had the Kataki Strom's dispositions filed away in his head, so they could swirl their wings and fly home.

One or two of the flutswods astride their birds, tough soldiers of the air, let rip a few pleasantries at thus turning tail. But their job was to escort the Prince Majister, not to tangle with benighted fluttrell-riders.

The recce patrol tamely flew back to camp.

Jumping off his bird and letting him be gathered up in the skilful hands of young Emin the Cheeky who couldn't wait until he was old enough to become a soldier and as a flutswod join the ranks of the aerial cavalry, Drak gave the graceful bird a gentle pat.

"Well done!"

"Aye, jis," quoth young Emin the Cheeky. "When you chose my Bright Feather you could not have chosen better."

Drak favored the lad with a smile and then said: "You keep him well-groomed. Your Bright Feather could sort out a whole squadron of those fluttrells before the second breakfast."

"What!" exclaimed Emin. "No, jis. Before the first breakfast!"

Drak laughed and took himself off to the tent where the chiefs of the army waited. He handed his spyglass to his orderly, Nath the Strict, for telescopes although relatively common and much-used were still valuable property needing care in use, and ducked his head to enter the tent.

He greeted the assembled chiefs and succinctly gave his impression of Yasi's host, the dispositions and his intentions.

Kapt Enwood nal Venticar, as the senior officer present, nodded his head and spoke first.

"The plan is good, jis. Since we have drawn him north our fortunes have changed. This day—well, this day may see a victory we can follow up."

The barrel-bodied man wearing simple pikeman's kit with the addition of a few discreet touches of gold here and there, and a cloak a trifle more scarlet than that generally allowed, cleared his throat. His face might have been constructed from weathered oak, old boots and black iron. His eyes, of good Vallian brown, were deeply sunk and his eyebrows grew like twin thorn-ivy hedges.

"Majister," he said in his gravelly voice. "Did you see anything of their phalanx?"

"I saw no pikemen, Brytevax Thandor. And I would prefer you to remember to address me as jis."

"Your command, jis!"

This man, Thandor Veltan ti Therfuing, this chunky, stubborn, immoveable Phalanx commander, had started out as a brumbyte in the files with the original Phalanx of Therminsax. He had gained recognition and promotion. Now he had been appointed brumbytevax, generally abbreviated to brytevax, to take command of Drak's phalangite force. He was known as Thandor the Rock.

The divisional commanders began to give their views, Drak listened, nodding from time to time. All of them recognized the importance of the intelligence. If that Kataki cramph did not have a phalanx force, the task this day would by that amount be less difficult. It would not be easy. By Vox, no, it would not be easy!

The army already in motion since before dawn would now move into those positions selected to give them the greatest advantage. Initial layout was highly important. With the phalanx force as the central pivot, Drak intended to refuse one wing and sweep the other around in a massive onslaught of everything he could spare. The air would be cleared by the flyers and the few airboats he had under command. Once the first contacts had been made and the light troops, the kreutzin, had done their work, and if Opaz Militant smiled on them this day, they should roll up Strom Yasi like a worn-out carpet.

Jiktar Endru and Jiktar Naghan the Bow, commanding the prince's bodyguard regiments, stood near the doorway, a part of the proceedings inside and a part of the constant watch kept outside.

Because his father's bunch of maniacs, called his juruk jikai, his guard corps, were organized in their own idiosyncratic way, Drak had to bare the throat to seeing different people representing the two regiments. They had some kind of rota system to choose commanders. He had representatives of the Emperor's Sword Watch and the Emperor's Yellow Jackets with him. One thing Drak did know. He'd not just far rather have them on his side than fight against them—he just wouldn't even think of fighting against them.

He looked about, raising his eyebrows.

Of no one in particular, he inquired: "Where is Leone Starhammer?"

An instant silence dropped down like a curtain. Then three or four spoke at once, and stopped. Drak looked puzzled. Now what the hell was going on?

He called across to Endru near the entrance. If anyone ought to know it ought to be commanders of the other two of his bodyguards.

"Endru?"

"Yes, jis. Leone has gone to greet Queen Lushfymi."

To Drak it appeared a volcano had gone off inside his head.

He opened his mouth, couldn't speak, shut his mouth. He swallowed. He looked balefully about. Then he got out a tithe of the words seething in him.

"Queen Lush! By Vox! Why does the woman have to choose the day of a battle to come visiting!"

Diplomatically, Endru rapped out: "It is clear she did not know a battle was due today."

"I don't know," said Drak, almost snarling. "I wouldn't put anything past her—and she is very, very welcome, of course. Always. Except—perhaps today. . . ."

No one in the tent cared to mention that the queen had been referred to by her nickname by the prince. The old emperor, whom Queen Lushfymi had hoped to marry, had said with great meaning that anyone who called her Queen Lush would have his or her head off. And he'd meant it.

For all that, in these latter days Queen Lush was the name by which most folk thought of Queen Lushfymi of Lome.

Drak scowled. He stuck his fist onto his rapier hilt and fiddled, an uncharacteristic gesture.

"Kapt Enwood, you'll have to take the right wing and I'll handle the left. Brytevax Thandor will command the center. By these means if the queen cannot be persuaded to watch the battle from a safe distance she will at least not be in the thick of it."

"With pleasure, jis!" exclaimed Enwood. He rubbed his hands. He'd thought he was in for a dull day. The plan called for the right wing to attack and the left to be refused.

"And not a word to the queen about the battle plan! Is that understood?"

"Understood, prince!" Everyone spoke up as though on parade.

Drak looked about on these people, folk he counted as friends and companions as well as loyal subordinates, all working for the good of Vallia. He could, had he wished, have become emotional. Instead, and without drawing his sword to bless them, he said: "Fight today with Vox to point and sharpen your weapons. May the light of Opaz go with you and your soldiers, every one. Remberee!"

"Remberee, prince!" they said, and then took their leave and went about the business of the day.

Nath the Strict came in with a tray bearing a cup of scalding hot Kregan tea and a silver plate of miscils and palines, all of which Drak tumbled down his gullet, not taking from the delicacies the enjoyment he should. His mind was plagued with doubts, which he knew he would throw off once the trumpets pealed the advance.

Concern for Queen Lush preyed on his mind.

His own small juruk jikai, consisting of Endru's PMSW and Naghan's PMDA, would see he came to no personal harm. Also, he was well aware that his father's bunch of madmen, ESW and

EYJ, although much preferring to be with the emperor, would take particular care of his son.

So that left Leone Starhammer's QLJV a free hand to care for the queen.

He had often heard his grandfather complaining about the way his people insisted on looking after him and standing in the way when the old devil wanted to get to handstrokes with the foe. His father, an even greater devil, said the same, even more vehemently. Now Drak understood much of those complaints.

If he told anyone of the bodyguards corps to go off and reinforce the right wing, as had been the original plan, they'd kick up an awful rumpus. They might not refuse; they'd make damn sure they were within striking distance of where he placed himself in the battle line.

Damn Queen Lush!

Then he felt remorse at his own churlishness.

She was a wonderful woman, who worked wholeheartedly for Vallia. Once her own country had been properly cleared of the flutsmen and slayers and aragorn who festered there, as they still did in the unliberated parts of Vallia, she would have to choose where to live. She would always be welcome in Vallia. Drak was sure of that.

Finishing the tea which as ever was the best drink a man could quaff, good honest Kregan tea, he snatched a handful of palines and quit the tent. There'd be strong wine for the swods in the ranks, for the soldiers deserved that, at the least.

Before him the army moved like a multi-colored

quilt spread over the ground. He enumerated off the formations, saw the flutter of flags, the treshes brilliant under the growing power of the suns. Armor and weapons glinted. Bands played. Nearer and in the center the three Kerchuris of the phalanx force sent up their paean, a strong solemn hymn to battle. Every now and again they'd change into a sprightly and usually risqué song, simply open-handed joyous ditties they'd sing as they marched forward into hell.

On the right of the line marched the First Vallia. The center was held by the Second Therminsax. Over on the left the Fifth Drak marched like a solid wall.

The Second had received their name from the town where the emperor had first created the phalanx. The Fifth were named for the half-man half-god mythical figure of Vallia's dim and legendary past. He, too, was thusly named.

The other Kerchuri of the Third Phalanx, the Sixth, were called the Sixth Delia. He wished they were with him today.

As for the Second Phalanx, up in the northeast past Hawkwa country, they consisted of the Third Opaz and the Fourth Velia.

He tried to brisk himself up as he mounted aboard his zorca, Happy Calamity. The days after the Battle of Corvamsmot were over. Alloran had won crushingly there. He'd had this blight mysteriously called Zankov with him then. In letters from his father and mother, Drak had been warned against this Zankov. The most disturbing item of news was that his younger sister

Dayra might be implicated with the fellow's misdeeds. There was a suspicion that he was acting as the paymaster for Alloran. Whatever the truth of all these rumors, one thing was known.

Zankov had slain the old emperor and blamed Drak's father, the new emperor. This slander was proved by Queen Lush, who knew the truth. At this memory Drak suddenly, overpoweringly, found himself longing for today never to happen.

If only. . . . If only he were back in Valka, or Delphond, riding zorcas in the wide plains below the Blue Mountains! If only he could give up the time necessary to study the old books . . . If only—well, he had a battle on his hands and a queen to cosset. A fugitive glimpse of Silda Segutoria's face and form passed before him, and he sighed, knowing if she were here they'd never keep her out of the hottest fighting.

His retinue closed up. Trumpeters, standard bearers, messengers, they were all tense, quivering, anticipating the excitements of the day. Also, they should expect the horrors. He rode out ahead, stony-faced, still and erect in the saddle.

The mass of soldiers ahead moving out with purpose, must act like a gigantic organism this day. They must crush Strom Rosil Yasi for good and press on through Ovvend and hurl into Kaldi and so reclaim all the mainland for Vallia.

One of his aides, beside himself with excitement, called out: "Jis! The queen!"

Drak turned his head and looked.

The blaze of color and glitter of gold and gems would fair blind anyone. Queen Lushfymi rode at the head of her regiment, with Leone and the high officers in close attendance. The queen rode a gray, and the zorca was so white as to appear ghostlike. The zorca's single spiral horn jutting from the center of her forehead was completely coated with gold leaf. Every scrap of harness was studded with gems. Drak was not so foolish as to suppose those jewels to be paste.

Queen Lush wore armor, golden armor, encrusted with gems. Enormous clouds of feathers floated over her helmet. She carried the usual arsenal of Kregan weapons, and spare weaponry as well. Drak didn't know if she looked splendid or foolish.

He tended to suspect she was absolutely splendid and only his own ill humor could make him think otherwise.

Her cavalcade halted, pushing his own folk a trifle to make room. Zorca hooves stamped. The suns glinted blindingly off armor and jewels and weapons. The strong sweet perfume of the women wafted across the small intervening space.

"Lahal, majestrix."

"Lahal, my dear Drak. I've come to make sure you poor silly dear that you don't get yourself killed."

Chapter Twelve

Of Water and of Blood

The manacles of iron, old and rusty, cut into his wrists cruelly. The fetters were of the same rusty antiquity and bit into his ankles. He was stripped naked. He hung suspended against a dismal brick wall, all running and slimy and green, and considered he was very hard done by. Very hard indeed.

The cell was small enough, in all conscience, and light entered through a barred opening high in a tunnel-like slot indicating ground level high above his head.

The jailers had, at the least, taken away the skeleton hanging on the opposite wall that had greeted San Fraipur when they'd dragged him down here. By the sacred radiance of Opaz! This was a dolorous place.

The jailers did feed him. One was a Gon, a tallish fellow rather stooped, with the bald shaven head of a Gon smothered in butter. The other was an apim, with half a left ear, a bent and broken nose, no teeth that were visible, and hands like claws. They fed him thin gruel, without honey, and crusts of bread green as grass. On this dreadful fare San Fraipur perforce kept body and ib together.

And why?

In the great and glorious name of Opaz—why?

Because he'd told Vodun Alloran the truth?

Or, perhaps, because that thing Arachna had so willed it?

"Return in four burs," King Vodun Alloran had said, "and give me the answers to my questions."

This Fraipur had done to the best of his ability.

He'd noticed, there in that stifling throne room with the black and green clad Katakis standing guard around the draped walls, that Alloran was flushed so that his face shone with sweat and passion. Since he had dismissed Fraipur he must have gone through some profound experience. So judged the sorcerer.

"Well, Fraipur! Speak out, man!"

No longer, then, the polite address as San. . . .

"I have given the question much thought. The forces with Strom Rosil are known, unless he has suffered another reverse."

Alloran didn't like that. With a sad and ugly feeling, for Fraipur had been devoted to this man, he recognized that he felt pleasure at his shaft.

"Go on, Fraipur. Tsleetha-tsleethi!"

"Yes, majister. The strengths of the Prince Majister are known only as to the last reports. I judge, and with reason, that he will receive reinforcements that will enable him to do more than resist the future advance of Strom Rosil." Fraipur hurried on. "If Kaldi is to be prevented from falling into the hands of Prince Drak, then we must send more troops."

Alloran leaned back. He looked pleased. "Yes?"

"That is the simple-minded reading of the situation, one any school child could arrive at."

"And?"

"Not and, majister, but. You would need to strip forces from their garrisons here in Rahartdrin. You would have to postpone the invasion of Tezpor and the other islands." Here he shot a hard look at the king. "You do remember, majister, what you have promised regarding Fruningen?"

Alloran roused himself in his throne. He leaned forward and his face blackened.

"You are insolent, Fraipur! What I choose to do with Fruningen, with any conquest, is mine alone to decide! Is that clear?"

"But, majister—Fruningen is small, a home for my friends, the teaching academies for the wizards—"

"If they are all as you are—well, never mind that. I will think on it. Go on with your answers."

Fraipur felt a drop of sweat plop off the end of his nose. He closed his eyes, opened them, and said: "What will happen is this, majister, if you decide to reinforce Strom Rosil Yasi against the Vallians—"

"I am the true Vallia!"

"Of course. Against the usurpers. They have

greater resources now, they have more regiments. You will be sucked in and overwhelmed—"

"I do not care for this, Fraipur!"

Fraipur struggled on.

"I judge the situation to be one for negotiation. If you hold Rahartdrin, the other islands, you will prove to be extremely hard to attack and dislodge. The sea crossing will be dangerous, and you have a fleet to protect the shores. Rather than lose many men in attempting to oust you, the emperor may come to terms, will recognize you—"

Alloran stood up. His face was a blot of anger.

"And I thought you a great mage! You are contemptible. You see nothing. Don't you understand I have many mercenaries sailing to join me? They come from North Pandahem, thousands of them. Soon I shall be so strong as to overwhelm this brat Prince Drak."

"The people—the usurpers—in Vondium know that. They have a fleet, in the air they are far more powerful than are you. They will take steps to prevent the paktuns from reaching you—"

"Enough! You have failed me yet again, Fraipur."

Alloran sat back on his throne. He put his chin on his right fist, gazing levelly at the sorcerer. His left hand began to run the rapier up and down in the scabbard.

"Tell me, what do you know of Water and of Blood?"

"Water and blood? Why, one you may drink with relish, the other not. One passes in to comfort, the other passes out to end it all. If there is a choice—"

"You prattle like an infant with a rattle in its teeth. I know the answer. I have been shown. Water is thin, not for a warrior. Blood is thick, and will slake a warrior's thirst. I choose blood!"

A conceit took Fraipur then, so that he was able to speak up.

"If you must choose between water and blood, majister, then my advice is to choose water. For the water represents the seas about Rahartdrin and the islands, which will wall you off in safety to come to terms with the emperor. The usurping emperor, to be sure. The blood will flow to everyone's ruin if you try to fight on the mainland."

So, here he was.

A famed Wizard of Fruningen strung up in rusty chains that were like to take his hands off soon. It was intolerable! His powers were real enough and he was confident he had read Alloran's riddle aright. That damned Arachna had told him that about the water and the blood. Well, the she leem, she'd been clever enough, seeing what was ahead, to cloak her answer so that the idiot Alloran brought his doom on his own head.

Oh, yes, Fraipur's powers were real enough; but they did not extend to getting him out of these chains and up that tunnel and through the iron-barred opening and out into the blessed fresh air of Kregen.

He closed his eyes and began to work his mind away from the pain in wrists and ankles, and the pain all over, come to that. He made himself think of the long scrubbed table at the academy on his island home of Fruningen, of the other lads all tussling and laughing and learning. He thought of the books, the lifs and the hyr lifs, of the scrolls. He thought of the mingled suns shine of Zim and Genodras. And he thought of the food the slaves brought out at meal times, which was attacked with such zest by the acolytes learning the arts to become Wizards of Fruningen.

Somehow or other, San Fraipur fabricated defenses against the madness-inducing situation in which he found himself.

Some distance away from Fraipur's miserable dungeon and considerably higher, Silda Segutoria sat polishing up her sword, the drexer glitteringly bright already, and thinking dark thoughts.

By Vox! This time she'd go armed to the teeth!

Still, poor old Lon the Knees. It was not really his fault. He lived in a parlous society, a heaving mass of humanity not far removed from the slaves. He'd have made enemies as well as friends. And, to be sure, she found herself warming to the bandy-legged fellow. He was a real character. Still and all, he had to produce Crafty Kando soon, or Silda Segutoria, if not Lyss the Lone, would blow up like a volcano in full eruption.

She strapped on the drexer on its individual belt alongside the rapier and shifted the various straps and fittings until they felt comfortable. The knapsack nestled on her left hip. She could dive her left hand in there in a jiffy, and she'd not cut herself up as that poor little spinlikl had done.

Her black leathers were soft and supple from skillful ministrations. Over her shoulders she swirled a dark plum-colored half-cloak. On her head, in place of the uniform helmet, or the lady's version of the universal Vallian floppy-brimmed hat, she slapped a charcoal-gray boltsch, a round hat fabricated from a feltlike material, flat and wide which could be pulled down fetchingly on one side. Within and padded to her head was a hard-boiled leather skull.

She'd bought the thing yesterday, it had cost two and a half silver stivers, and she'd ripped out the bright yellow and green feathers. No doubt the hat represented plunder, for the feathers were not local. No doubt, also, that was why she'd been able to haggle down to two and a half. The thing was worth a trifle more than that.

The schturval* of Rahartdrin, now officially extinguished by King Vodun, was yellow and green with two diagonal red slashes, together with a lotus flower.

Making sure everything was shipshape and Vallian fashion, she stomped out in her tall black boots.

Perhaps, this time, she could arrange what amounted to a meeting between two worlds.

High life and low life having failed, she'd fallen

*Schturval: The emblem entire consisting of colors and symbol considered as an entity.—A.B.A.

back on the sensible person's course of action and gone for religion.

All folk tended to have one chief god in whom they reposed trust and confidence, although some of the horrors called religions in Havilfar created sheer terror in the believers. As well as Opaz, chiefest among the spirits, the light of the Invisible Twins made manifest, Vallians gave their allegiance to a bewildering variety of other gods, godlings, goddesses and spirits.

Vox stood in a category apart; from being the favorite of the warriors Vox had spread into universal use.

Mind you, said Silda to herself as she marched briskly along in the midafternoon suns light, all these temples gave openings for a whole slew of priests and priestesses to wax fat on the credulous. Cities claimed precedence very often on economic, military or political grounds. The factor of the number of temples within a city could never be ignored. The city with more temples than its neighbor always made its citizens feel they had scored heavily even before any argument began.

Rashumsmot, as its name indicated, was a town and not a city. If King Vodun decided to stay on here he might well build and enlarge the place and call it Rashumsden. He would have little need of inviting new priests, temples and godlings into his new city, for Rashumsmot was already lavishly provided, as any self-respecting town must be, with a splendiferous array of places of worship.

"The Temple of Applica the Bounteous," she'd told Lon, most firmly. "I don't give a damn if Crafty Kando thinks Applica is a fat old besom. Just get him there. The Day is the Day of Applica Conceived, so there will be crowds."

"But, Lyss—"

"It's hard enough to arrange my off-duty to coincide with the whims of your friend. By Vox, Lon! Time's a-wasting."

"Yes, Lyss . . ."

So, here she was, a plum-colored cloak swirled about her black leathers concealing her weaponry, a hat pulled over one ear, striding off to the half-ruined temple of a fat old lady goddess who oversaw the production of twins—if you believed that, of course.

The temple had not suffered too badly and had not burned. The roof over the priestess's quarters had been stoved in, no doubt by an airboat falling on it, and they had shifted the acolytes out of their rooms to take them over. The main area lay open, fronting five tall columns and a broad flight of steps whereon the priestesses performed. The congregation was composed of a wide variety of people, three quarters of them women. The most noticeable common denominator was that they were pregnant.

Lon spotted Silda and trotted over and they stood in the shadows of the first interior wall, shoulder high, to watch. Lon quivered.

"There he is. And Lop-eared Tobi's with him, too."

Following Lon's inconspicuous gesture, Silda

saw the two men. Crafty Kando appeared much as he had when he'd put his nose into The Leather Bottle. His companion had made some attempt to smarten himself up to visit the temple, and still contrived to look an unhanged ruffian, bad teeth, pocked skin and stringy hair and all.

Two worlds, meeting on neutral territory, said Silda to herself, and sighed, and thrust away weak thoughts of happier days and places where she'd rather be right now.

Incense smoke drifted across, mingling with the choked smells of the mass of people. Many were kneeling. They were being led through the rites of the service by the priestesses and chanted and responded to order. Crafty Kando and Lop-eared Tobi eased across and Lon moved forward by the low wall to speak with them. Silda waited. At last Lon turned, smiling, and Silda walked over to join them.

The pappattu was made quickly, informally, and Silda, about to broach the subject burning uppermost in her mind now she'd actually made contact with the thief, saw over his shoulder a woman in a brown dress beckoning to someone hidden beyond a pillar. Before Silda spoke she saw a bull-necked swaggering fellow step out from beyond the pillar. By his black brows alone she would have recognized him as Ortyg the Kaktu. The last time she'd seen him in The Dancing Flea she'd knocked him down. Well, well, now. . . .

Without more ado Ortyg hurled his knife and then whipped out his sword and charged. The knife thudded into the wood trim of the corner as Silda shoved Crafty Kando out of the way. Four other men ran in the wake of Ortyg the Kaktu. He knocked over a pregnant woman kneeling in his way. His face was black with passion.

"I'll have you now, rast, cramph, vermin!"

The three men with Silda swung about sharply, and exclamations unfit for utterance in a temple fell from their lips. Silda didn't bother with any of that. Out came her rapier in a twinkling and the main gauche, the Jiktar and the Hikdar. She leaped forward. Ortyg recognized her. His scowling face broke into a dazzling smile, black teeth and all, and he fairly howled down.

Silda had no time to waste. This was not the time for pretty expositions of the art of the sword. Anyway, Ortyg was out to kill them all, that was clear, and she could not afford to take risks, for herself or for Lon.

So she took the clumsy blow along the left-hand dagger, stuck Ortyg through the guts, withdrew, slashed the next fellow down the face, came back into line to stick the third in the eye. The fourth was gasping up blood around the knife in his throat. Lon started forward.

"I'll buy you a new knife, Lon. Run!"

Incontinently, the four of them ran out of the uproar spreading within the Temple of Applica the Bounteous.

They didn't stop running and then walking swiftly until they were past the Street of Krokan the Glorious where they could ease down and catch their breath. Of them all, Lop-eared Tobi whooped in the most gasps and wheezes. Silda's breathing was scarcely troubled.

"By Diproo the Nimble-Fingered!" said Kando. "What she-cat have you found yourself this time, Lon?"

Chapter Thirteen

To smash a dragon's egg

King Vodun Alloran found he was most vexed with himself for being troubled over San Fraipur, the Wizard of Fruningen. Fraipur had served Alloran's father and then himself with devotion and expertise, his advice sound and well-judged. What troubled King Vodun was simply that he could not make up his mind if Fraipur should be killed out of hand, left to rot in his dungeon, tortured to death or smothered. And, if torture was decided on, then Alloran would have to make his choice of the various alternatives the torture masters could offer. Yes, it was a vexing question.

"By the Triple-Tails of Targ the Untouchable!" he burst out. "I'll throw the problem to Five-handed Eos Bakchi."

At his outburst the Kataki guards around the walls swiveled their narrow demonic eyes upon him. He was apim, not Kataki, yet he used Kataki oaths. He continued to call upon the name of

Opaz in public, for Arachna counseled him it was as yet unwise to move too rapidly. He certainly counted himself the most fortunate of men that he had discovered her and that she had entered his service. The Katakis served him well.

There was a time, he remembered, when he loathed Katakis with their bladed whiptails and their slaving ways, but that was before Arachna had opened his eyes.

He gave his orders to his chamberlain Naghan the Chains and in due time four husky fighting men were wheeled in. Each was naked. All were apim. They stared about, dazzled by the magnificence all around, nervous yet relieved that they had not been thrown to the wild animals or sold off as slaves.

Chin propped on fist, Alloran studied them. Yes, they looked evenly matched; he would not take a certain bet on any one of them. Eos-Bakchi, spirit of chance, would decide.

As the men stood huddled and limp with dawning apprehension, Alloran's serving girls tied colored ribbons about the men's left arms. White for smothering. Red for death. Green for torture. Black for rotting. Each man was handed a Vallian dagger, long, slender and lethal.

"Fight!" commanded Alloran. "All against all in mélée. The winner will gain his life." To himself, he added with a sly self-pleasing humor: "And if he is in respectable condition, the honor of Arachna!"

The men fought.

Afterward slaves cleared away the mess and

swabbed the floor and the man wearing the black arm band, streaming blood, was carried off in a blanket. He still lived. Him, Alloran made the promise, he would reward by a visit to savor the honor of Arachna.

With that tiresome problem out of the way, he could turn to the question of building this wonderful new phalanx his people had promised him. He knew the Phalanx of Vallia, and understood that Strom Rosil mayhap did not. With the thousands of mercenaries flooding in from North Pandahem, funded by Zankov's gold, he would crush the usurpers and then begin the great march on Vondium.

The phalanx he was building would be a vital component of his army. He sat back and held up his hand and a sprite in silver gauze placed a golden goblet therein. Alloran drank. Life was going to be good and get better, by Takroti!

When everything was prepared he was informed by a Mantissa and went through into the inner chamber. All proceeded as before, except that the man was a Fristle. When Arachna threw back the cloak the golden furry body of a Fristle fifi drove the breath thick and clogging into Alloran's throat. The tail-hand crept out along the bed, took up the snake-curved dagger and thrust the blade deeply into the Fristle's vitals. The mingled shriek of agony and ecstasy, the blood and the limp falling away, and Arachna spoke in those husky cobwebbed tones reaching in through mazy distances.

"If you do not wish to be eaten by the dragon, you must smash the egg in the nest."

Pondering Arachna's words, Alloran walked slowly from the secret chamber, through his throneroom without pausing and so on toward the top floor of the west wing.

Naghan the Chains hovered, and to him Alloran said, "Fetch food and wines for the lady Chemsi and me."

"At once, majister, at once."

Just before Naghan hurried off Alloran snapped out: "And find Scauron the Gaunt and send him to me."

"Your command, majister."

Scauron the Gaunt, decided King Vodun as he strode off to share a pleasant meal and company with his light o' love, was the perfect tool for smashing dragon's eggs.

Three victories having taken the Prince Majister of Vallia across the province of Ovvend to the borders of the kovnate of Kaldi, he paused there to consider the next steps. The first victory, Vongleru, had been hard fought, as expected. The second, Ondorno, gained slightly more readily. The most recent battle had seen the Vallian forces routing their opponents at Naghan the Folly's Ford with convincing ease.

All the same, Drak was under no illusions that the war was won. He could not just march his army across Kaldi without a by your leave. The Kataki Strom was reeling back with a bloody nose; he was a long way from being beaten.

Also, Prince Drak must take careful thought for the other fronts in Vallia. Up in the northeast they were having continual trouble and an army containing the whole of the Second Phalanx swatted this way and that. He could expect, at least for the moment, no reinforcements from there. Up in the central portions of the island Kov Turko fought for his province against Layco Jhansi and also against the Racters. Turko had the Fourth Phalanx consisting of the Seventh Lela and the Eighth Seg, two Kerchuris who were seeing a lot of action. Turko would rather be asking for more men than releasing them to fight elsewhere.

In the capital, the Lord Farris and the Presidio ran the country in the absence of the emperor and the Prince Majister, and loyal and competent they were, too, thank Opaz! They were in the business of raising fresh troops. But soldiers, saddle animals and flyers, artillery, weaponry, did not grow on trees or sprout from the ground.

Pacing restlessly up and down inside his tent, jurukkers on guard outside, abstaining from wine until the hour grew on, Drak pulled at his lower lip and struggled with the decisions he must make. As for Queen Lushfymi—the woman was a treasure and a jewel, no doubt of that. She had behaved herself during the battles, and had come to no harm. Her conversation, easy, educated, witty, turned on topics increasingly concerned with the desirability of Drak, as the putative emperor, finding a wife and thus ensuring the succession. No doubt was left in anyone's mind, least of all in Drak's, that he was expected to choose Queen Lushfymi of Lome. After all, she outshone all other women, did she not?

Well, pondered Drak, cut by guilt and memories, well. . . .

He heard the sentries bellow the ritual challenge: "Llanitch!" Anyone ordered to "Halt!" quite like that halted at once, otherwise they'd be shafted. Then the tent flap was thrown back. Drak half-turned, expecting to see a sentry barging in to announce whoever the visitor was, and he saw a lithe and limber young lady, clad in russet leathers, a rapier and main gauche at her hips, a long evil-looking whip curled up over her shoulder, a plain bag with red stitching slung so that she could dive her left hand into it without thought. Her face glowed at him, mischievous, beautiful with that familiar heartbreaking beauty he knew so well, yet fierce, dominating, and haunted by some inner conflict not yet resolved.

"Drak, you old shaggy sea-leem, you!"

"Dayra! You little monkey! What in a Herrelldrin Hell are you doing here?"

Brother and sister clasped each other, old sores forgotten, joying in seeing each other again. Life in the turbulent world of Kregen drives folk apart and makes reunions all the more joyful.

Presently Drak said, "Now you are here it is appropriately enough the time for wine."

"Assuredly, brother. But a mouthful only for me. I must fly on sharpish."

"Oh?"

They sat side by side on the sprawl of cushions on the floor and Dayra took the goblet of wine.

"Yes. I'm flying to Hamal. It's about time I saw Lela again and I want to size up this bright new prince of hers."

"I hear Prince Tyfar of Hamal is a splendid fellow."

"So I hear. I want to see for myself. And you know he calls her Zia. That's because father and he knew her as Jaezila. Father calls her that nearly all the time instead of Lela. Mother sometimes despairs of him, I tell you."

They talked on, exchanging news, happy that now they could talk thus without the black memories of the past intruding. Dayra just said, almost in passing: "Zankov is dead, or I think he must be, seeing that Cap'n Murkizon broke his backbone across."

Drak took up his wine, drinking to cover the pause for consideration. Whatever the troubles with that bastard Zankov may have been, Dayra possessed a bright spirit that reacted emotionally and which might not be altogether rational still. He was just about to make some noncommittal remark when Dayra went on speaking as though the subject had not been brought up.

"Oh, and Drak, you great fambly, when are you and Silda to be married? I cannot understand why you are leaving it so late."

Because he was so genuinely glad to see this wayward sister who had caused such concern to the family and heartache for his mother, he refused to become stupidly pompous and indignant. He swallowed the wine.

"It is not arranged in any way that I shall marry Silda."

"There, you see!" flamed Dayra, known as Ros the Claw. "Why is it that *you* shall marry *her*? Why is it not that Silda hasn't decided to marry you? Because you are a man?"

"No, you fambly—I apologize. I have to remember to think like the Prince Majister who may someday be emperor. Surely you recognize that? As for Silda—I think she would marry me if—"

"Would! If! Why, you insufferable onker! She loves you!"

"Yes."

"Well, then—?"

When Drak did not answer, Dayra burst out: "It's this fat Queen Lush! That's it, isn't it?"

"Well, Dayra, look—"

"Since I've been back with the family—or at least those who've been around—I've learned a few surprising things. Anyway, what about Uncle Seg? What about mother and father? Oh, I know you can't marry someone because your folks think you should, but, Drak, dear—Queen Lush!"

"She is a remarkable woman—"

"Of course."

They both sat silently after that, the air as it were, exhausted between them.

Then Dayra, very much Ros the Claw, snapped out: "Anyway, where is Silda now?"

"I've no idea."

"You've no idea! By Vox! What a brother I have."

Studying this stern, sober, upright brother of hers, Dayra saw that perhaps, just perhaps, he might be overawed by this Queen Lush and her magnificence and undoubted beauty and worldly-wise ways. She wasn't really fat, of course not, just a trifle on the plump side. She might, in Drak's eyes who must think of himself as an emperor one day, far outdo Silda Segutoria in those qualities deemed necessary in an empress. Also, and this thought bore a great deal of truth, Drak might be more than a little offput by what he knew of the Sisters of the Rose. Their father might go off on mysterious jaunts; but so did their mother the Empress Delia. Any woman who was a sister of the SOR could expect to work for the Order, and be absent from the hearth and home.

Equality in Vallia, as was not true in some countries of Paz, cut both ways.

Slowly, unhappy at what he felt he must say, Drak wet his lips and said, "Look, Dayra. I must say that really this is my business—"

"You mean you think it is no concern of mine!" She flared it out, scornful, brilliant of color, her eyes marvels in the soft samphron oil lamps' glow. "I tell you, brother, it is of great consequence to me. Not just because Silda is a dear friend. Not just because you will be emperor one day and must have the very best empress possible. Not just because Queen Lush for all her magnificence is pathetic. No, by Vox, Drak! Because I'm choosy about who is to be my sister-in-law, that's why!"

"I think—"

"Yes! You are right, by Chozputz!" She stood up like a flame in the light, stamped her tall black boots on the carpet, looped her evil whip about her shoulder. "I'm going!"

"Dayra—please—it shouldn't—"

"By Chusto, Drak! D'you take me for a ninny! I can't stay lollygagging about here. I'll be back. I want to see Jilian, among others. Give my remembrances to those here who knew me. Remberee!"

She was gone like a tornado before Drak collected his wits. "Remberee," he called after her, feeling a fool.

Outside the tent checking on the guard, Jiktar Endru Vintang slammed himself up to rigid attention. The swirl of russet leathers, a swift: "Thank you, Jik. Remberee," and the princess was away astride her flutduin. He sighed. He wouldn't relish being wed to that one—and yet, and yet . . . !

He saw Hikdar Carlotta walking across from the queen's guard detail and decided to hang around for a time. Carlotta was a jolly, red-cheeked girl with a good humor for everyone except a sloppy soldier. He smiled as she approached in the torch's streaming light.

The prince whom Endru guarded snatched up a goblet of wine, drained it, and hurled the thing at the floor. Women! Sisters! Queens! They were enough to drive a man into the claws of Mak Chohguelm the Ib-Cracker!

Anyone observing Prince Drak act like this would have been astounded.

He had to sort out his private life, yet there was never enough time to handle all the affairs pressing him. He was somberly aware that each time he made a mistake men and women died. A carpenter might make a table with one leg shorter than the other and the table wobbled. What a pity. The Prince Majister made the wrong decision and regiments could be cut down. That, to Drak, seemed too monstrous even to be encompassed by pity.

Troubled as all hell he saw a girl with a white shawl wrapped about slender shoulders and hair unbound sidle into the tent. She put a finger to her lips. Endru must have let her pass. He did not know her.

"Majister. The queen craves an immediate and private meeting. You must come at once—"

"Is the queen ill? Has evil befallen her?"

"No, majister. Hurry!"

Alarmed, Drak snatched up his belts where his rapier and dagger swung scabbarded and followed the girl out of the tent.

What jumped demonically into his mind was monstrous and totally unthinkable. Wasn't it?

Chapter Fourteen

Deviltry under the Moons

They were a right rapscallion bunch. They met in the damp and tumbledown house of Yolande the Gregarian because Silda was tired of trying to meet where fights kept erupting. She had provided silver to buy wine and food and she wanted to complete her orders before they all fell down paralytic. When the time came, she promised herself, there'd be damn little if any wine, by the broken teeth and oozing eyes of Sister Melga the Harpy Herself!

"Well, I dunno," said Crafty Kando, sounding most cool.

"It's against reason," said Rundle the Flatch, a low-browed, tangle-haired fellow with half an ear missing.

"Since when, Rundle," said Lon the Knees, taking a handful of palines from the red pottery dish, "have you and reason been on speaking terms?"

As Rundle started to bristle up, Long Nath said: "But against the king? It'd be like washing away the Rahart Mountains with one cup of water."

"By Dipsha the Nimble-fingered!" exclaimed Yolande the Gregarian. "What do you know about washing, Long Nath? When was the last time you washed?"

"I'll have you know—"

"There's gold in it," cut in Lon. He continued to wonder what the hell he'd got himself into with this glorious girl; but he was in and wasn't going to back out now. "Lots of gold."

"Well, gold, now . . ." And: "There's ways and ways . . ." And: "He's for the chop, that one, anyway, by Black Chunguj!" They argued, as it were, to clear their minds and to gain sustenance one from the other.

Looking at this unlikely gang of cutthroats, Silda understood that a Sister of the Rose used whatever tools came to hand suitable for her purpose.

Lop-eared Tobi could still hear the shuddersome thud of that knife as it struck the wood instead of embedding itself in his back. Or Crafty Kando's back. He owed this girl his life, at the least.

"You call him king," spoke out Lop-eared Tobi. "But he's no more than a thief like us."

"I never stole from Kovneva Rashumin," said Ob-eye Mantig, with a shake of his head and such droll seriousness that the others laughed at him.

"We would be," said Lon carefully, "taking back what rightfully belongs to Rahartdrin."

No one there dreamed that, if they succeeded, they'd return the gold to the kovneva. There were limits, by Diproo the Nimble-fingered!

Useless to try to browbeat these people. They knew what they knew and understood their trade. Silda took a paline from the dish and before speaking held the little yellow berry between her fingers.

"I understood that you were masters of your art. But, of course, if you do not have the skills required—"

They broke out into uproar at this, their professional thieves' competence questioned. Crafty Kando quieted them. He looked at Silda meaningfully.

"You have not told us, my lady, why you wish to burgle the king's gold."

"Why not? It is not his, as we have said. And he is bad for the country. We all know that."

"That is sooth. The kovneva was different. Times were good in those days."

Silda knew enough from what her father had told her about Katrin Rashumin to know that having lost her husband the kov, Katrin had allowed her island to fall into a disreputable state through bad management and incompetent and mercenary managers. The emperor had helped her sort out her problems. Rahartdrin had prospered until the Times of Troubles.

The people of Rahartdrin, the Rahartese, would dearly love to throw King Vodun Alloran off their island back to his own province of Kaldi. They might do more, given the opportunity. But no one was unaware of the drably clad men and women with their crossbows who seemed to be everywhere. Spies, too, had to be looked out for, and Silda felt thankful that everyone in this gathering had been vouched for.

No one it appeared to Silda was as yet fully convinced. Crafty Kando raised a point of great importance.

"My lady, are there Pachaks among the guards?"

"No."

So that cleared away one obstacle, for Pachaks are notorious for the honor and zealousness with which they discharge their duties when hired on as guards. Pachaks, with their straw yellow hair and two left arms, one right arm and powerful tail hand, give their nikobi and will not desist from the honorable course until they are discharged by their employer or by death.

Silda did not mention that there would almost certainly be Katakis. A way around that problem had to be found.

Yolande the Gregarian stood up. A strong woman plump with muscle, she had buried four husbands and was on the lookout for a fifth. Her face showed signs of her struggles with life. Very deft with a loop of rope, this Yolande. At first she had vehemently if privately detested this new supple stripling of a girl; but when she realized that Lyss the Lone had no designs on the men in Yolande's life, she welcomed Lyss as a female companion among the men.

"My loyalty remains with Kovneva Katrin. I

will go up against this new despicable king. Also, I need the gold, for I shall marry again soon."

This latter remark caused more concern among the men present than Yolande's other decision. Silda seized her chance, spoke briefly and eloquently, cast a look at Lon and lapsed into silence.

Now the decision rested with Five-handed Eos-Bakchi.

Drak followed the girl in the white shawl out of his tent. The sentries saluted. He saw Endru talking to one of the queen's guards and called across: "Endru. I am to see the queen. You need not turn out the men."

"Quidang!"

Endru and Carlotta watched the prince and the girl walk toward the queen's tent.

Torchlight pooled around the tents. The ever-present murmurous noise of an army even at night floated in from the camp. Carlotta and Endru resumed their conversation.

The white-shawled girl and Drak vanished into the darkness between the two pools of light.

"I suppose, my famous kampeon," said Carlotta, joking Endru for whom she had a deep respect, "you fancy that chit of a girl instead of a jurukker like me."

"Why, Carlotta!" Endru put on a show of gallantry. "You malign me cruelly. Anyway, who is she? I have never seen her before."

"Nor have I. The queen is highly choosy about the girls who serve her. I saw little of this one in the torchlight; but she looked beautiful, as I'm sure you noticed. The queen does not often have really beautiful young girls about her person."

Carlotta saw no need to give the reason for that.

Looking at the queen's tent in its sheath of light and the Jikai Vuvushis on guard there, Endru waited for the girl and the prince to appear. He'd have a careful look at her. Prospects might be improving. . . . He waited expectantly.

Presently, he said, "Where are they?"

Before Carlotta had time to answer, Endru bellowed at his men. The shock hit him like a thunderclap.

"Turn out the guard! Alarm! Follow me!"

He ran like a maniac for the darkness between the tents.

Carlotta, abruptly aware of the situation, shrilled: "Bring lights!" and took off after Endru.

Past those pools of light the night clamped down with only one of Kregen's lesser moons vaulting past. The starlight did nothing to assist Endru's eyes, still dazzled by the torches. He ran on, blinking, whipping out his sword, trying to see.

The horror he experienced drove him on. The prince, who considered him as a friend, depended on him. And he had failed him! He ran on dementedly.

A vague shape ahead . . . ? The fugitive starlight wink of a blade . . . ? Endru peered ahead. That was the petal shape of an airboat. Figures, dark and ominous, clustered below and then he saw the sudden blob of white rising up against the flank of the flier.

That was the white shawl of that Opaz-forsaken girl!

They had been duped. The prince was in mortal peril. Endru shouted, screaming, and ran on headlong. Carlotta, up with him now, fleetly running, saw what was going on. Her sword snouted. Together, they rushed on as the last figures clambered aboard the airboat. It began to rise.

A lump and then another showed above the bulwarks.

Endru felt nothing. One moment he was running on, the next he was pitching forward, flat on his face, with the crossbow bolt through him. He tried to yell, and froth and blood bubbled. Carlotta fell on top of him. He tried to push her off and she felt like all the Mountains of the North. He stared up as his men reached him, swords and spears brandished, and saw the airboat rise and turn and, as his eyes misted over, she vanished into the shadows.

King Vodun Alloran beamed. He felt the glow of pleasure all through him. Chemsi the Fair had not been treating him just lately as he considered a king should be treated, and she had packed her baggage and been seen off. Just where she'd been sent, Alloran did not inquire. He was too wrapped up in his new light o' love, Thelda the Voluptuous.

And, on top of his new conquest—this!

With deep, delicious delight coursing all through him, King Vodun Alloran stared down upon the bound and unconscious body of Drak, Prince Majister of Vallia.

"You have done well, Scauron the Gaunt. Exceedingly well."

"If I have served you, majister—"

Alloran's wits were quick enough.

"What, fambly, that will requite you? No gold, then?"

Caught out, Scauron bowed. "I am at the command of the king, majister."

"Good. Then get this proud prince sent into the custody of the Mantissae. Tell them that never have they been offered a choicer morsel. No, by Takroti, never!"

Again, Scauron bowed, and started on his duties. He accepted orders and carried them out. He didn't much care for all the Katakis thronging about Alloran. But he did know, as they say on Kregen, to keep his hat on in the rain.

Frightened slaves carried the limp form of the prince through side corridors from the anteroom where Scauron the Gaunt had delivered him to the king. Drak was passed on through a triply guarded doorway into the clutching claws of the Mantissae.

Chapter Fifteen

Tells of a wisp of straw

Although the darkness was not that of a night of Notor Zan—when no moons shine in the skies of Kregen—the Maiden with the Many Smiles would be late, and only a lesser moon raced across the starfields. The night breeze whispered along the cobbled alleyways of Rashumsmot. Lights flickered erratically. This was a night for ghosties and ghoulies to prowl the shadowed streets seeking soft throats and warm blood. Silda Segutoria firmly ensconced in the persona of Lyss the Lone, threw off these childish fancies.

She had put in a great deal of hard work on Crafty Kando's nefarious band. They were not drikingers, bandits, but they were a cutthroat crew. At the smell of gold, a number of newcomers had been recruited by Kando, all men and women he certified as safe.

Between them and under Silda's guidance they had scouted the back areas of the villa and Kando had pronounced no difficulty in getting into the grounds. These folk had their ways of avoiding sentries. But, to get into the building itself was an altogether different kettle of fish. Silda had rejected any ideas of introducing this hairy bunch into the normal entrances. They'd not be chucked out on their ears immediately. Oh, no. They'd be rounded up at the points of spears and sold off as slaves.

So she was forced to arrange a break-in. All the ordinary windows would be no use. Many of the men in the gang were accomplished bar breakers or benders, and others specialists in door-opening. If Silda's plan was to work, these folk were of paramount importance. The other important side of this operation nearly caused the whole show to come to grief.

"Swords?" said Lop-eared Tobi. His voice did not so much quaver as shrill in alarm.

"Swords?" yelped Long Nath. "Oh, no!"

"But," said Silda, nonplused. "If we meet up with sentries—"

"Run, or loop 'em, or the knife," quoth Yolande the Gregarian. The meeting, the last before Silda felt herself fully committed, being held at Yolande's crumbling house again provided remarkable calm after earlier attempts at meetings. "Or," added Yolande, "a short spear, perhaps."

"Very well," snapped Silda. "I will provide short spears. By Vox! I thought you'd have handled swords in your lives."

"Oh, no, my lady. Swords are not for the likes of us."

So, outfitted as a gang of thieves with the addition of short spears purloined from the armory by Lyss the Lone, they'd set off. And the night was dark.

Silda, a Sister of the Rose, needed no assistance in scaling the outer wall. She was as adept as any of the skulkers at skulking. A funny little thought hit her that Dayra, or Jilian, would joy to be with her now. They prowled on toward the wall of the villa, shrouded in darkness, and if there were any sentries in this quarter their presence was not made known.

Crafty Kando said between his teeth: "Wait here."

He slid off with a few of his people to check the last approaches across a greensward. Silda with the others waited in shrubbery. The night pressed down.

Presently, Kando returned. His whisper breathed like a furtive slipper on polished wood.

"The damned windows are all boarded up. Bricked up. You promised us an entrance, my lady."

"Let me have a look." Silda was fed up with handing about. "There are windows all along the wall here."

She and Kando slid ahead, ghostlike through the darkness. Kando had to acknowledge that this fine lady certainly knew how to skulk. They reached the wall and in the dimness Silda saw two windows bricked up.

"They are all like this at the back," said Kando.

"What about those?" Silda indicated windows

set in the angle of wall and ground. "They are barred, yes. Does that prevent you?"

"No, But they must lead below ground."

"And a good place to start. I'll get the rest of the people. You start."

Silda, without more ado, started back for the shrubbery.

A voice from out of the darkness said, "Silda."

She stopped as though shot through by a crossbow bolt.

"Silda!"

Her first thought was that this must be Mandi Volanta out on sentry go. But that voice—she knew whose voice that was. . . .

Off to the side and hidden from observation from Kando at the wall and the others in the shrubbery a yellow light bloomed. That glow looked for all the world like the radiance from a samphron-oil lamp. She ran silently straight for the glow, halting, peering, saying, "Deb-Lu!"

"Yes, Silda, my dear, it is me. There is very little time. Drak—"

Silda felt her heart contract. "What of Drak?"

"He needs you help. You defended him against the clansmen and would have given your life. The emperor used his skill with the Krozair longsword through my arts in gladiomancy. You remember, Silda, up there in Ithieursmot in Northern Jevuldrin?"

"I remember."

Deb-Lu-Quienyin, a magical and mystically powerful Wizard of Loh, did not really stand in the garden of King Vodun's villa in Rashumsmot.

Deb-Lu could be anywhere in Vallia. In his plain robes with his funny old turban that was forever falling over one ear, he was bathed in the lamp's glow, here in the darkness of a single-moon night!

Silda was vaguely aware that the two Wizards of Loh exerted their thaumaturgical powers in defense of their comrades. She had never considered the matter over much. Now Deb-Lu-Quienyin rattled on passionately.

"I will try to guide you, Silda. Drak has been taken by the madman Alloran. He is to be sacrificed, and there is sorcery involved. My arts—such as they are—are at you disposal. But I must work through a—well, never mind that. Choose the fifth window from the right end of the villa, and break through. And, Silda—hurry!"

"I will, I will. Drak—"

"By Hlo-Hli, Silda. Run!"

The eerieness of this confrontation, the insubstantial wraith-form of the wizard, projected by the power of his kharrna for miles and miles through thin air, could not be allowed to affect her. She fairly flung herself on, calling in a low penetrating voice. The people from the shrubbery came out, warily, casting glances in every direction. They did not see the Wizard of Loh.

At the wall Silda, impatiently, said, "Break through the fifth window from the right. And hurry."

"Now wait a minute," said Kando, standing up. He'd been working on the first window. "Why—?"

"There's no time to argue. The fifth window."

Crafty Kando saw the girl meant what she said. One window or the next, so what was the difference? He got his people started on breaking a way in. Expert at their tasks, they had the bars out and a rope down and then all eyes turned on Silda. She didn't hesitate. She grabbed the rope, put her booted feet into the chutelike opening and slid down. The darkness and the stench hit her as though she'd plummeted into Cottmer's Caverns.

Deb-Lu's voice whispered, "Tell them to wait."

She called up the slot, "Wait!"

Another voice, faint, husky with soreness, said, "What? Who's there?"

"We have come to save you in return for a favor," said the ghostly apparition of Deb-Lu, now faintly visible. He must have turned down his lamp so that his shrewd friendly features, highlighted, took on that upwardly shadowed aura of omnipotent power. He did not look the cheerful, pottering old buffer Silda knew and loved. Now he looked what he truly was, one of the most powerful mages in all of Kregen.

"I am chained and helpless—"

"You will soon be set free. In return you must use your powers, aided by mine, to guide my friends. We seek a certain person whose value to us is immense. I am sure you understand the nature of our bargain."

"You are a Wizard of Loh?"

"Yes."

"Then, San, I must agree and place my ib under the hand of Opaz into your protection. I will do as you command."

"Thank you, San Fraipur."

A wisp of straw among the dire scatterings on the floor lifted, it seemed of its own accord, rose into the air. It curved toward Silda and she took it into her hand.

"When San Fraipur is free, give him the talisman. There is power therein. He will know how to use it. I have done what I can for now. There are portents in Vallia, werewolves to be dealt with. Time is running out. Hurry!"

The glow faded and Deb-Lu was gone.

"Come down!" Silda called up the tunnel slot.

Lon the Knees was first down. He made a face at the smell and then started to strike a light. Kando and the others followed, and although they crowded the cell, they made no more noise than the schrafters in their hidden recesses gnawing on dead men's bones.

As they started in on the job of freeing Fraipur, two men appeared at the cell opening, took one look, and tried to flee. One was a butter-head Gon, the other an apim with half a left ear. Both were hit on the head with just sufficient force to put them to sleep. They were bound.

Silda gave Fraipur the wisp of straw. Truth to tell, she could feel no difference in the straw; but Fraipur took it up and in the covered-lantern glow she could see him as it were swell, grow taller. He put on the unconscious apim's rough clothes and without a word immediately led off out of the cell. Silda felt a rush of confidence.

The layout of the villa as it had been in the past was known in the thieves fraternity and Silda was able to indicate the likely places where Alloran had altered walls and made doors to create his scret apartments in the rear. There was no certainty about any of that, of course; but common sense told her that if she went up and remained in the rear she would emerge beyond that mysterious gold-framed green velvet door. She urged the band on with vigor, and San Fraipur, talisman in hand, went in the van.

With shielded lights they went up the stairs, broke quietly through a locked door, and so came into a carpeted corridor. Fraipur unhesitatingly turned right.

He felt gripped in the talons of a power so much greater than his own that it was like being swept away in a tidal wave. He was content to keep his side of the bargain and then, afterwards, he would have to think about his future. As for Alloran, Fraipur now knew he did not care what happened to that evil man.

No one appeared to inhabit this corridor and the rooms at each side were merely bedrooms with little of value. The gang pressed on. Fraipur did pick up a long curved knife.

The passage ended at a green velvet door.

"Open that, and quietly," ordered Silda. "We are bound to find a few guards on the other side. You need not be gentle with them."

When the door had been swiftly and expertly opened, the first through were Silda and Lon, side by side.

They found themselves in a small anteroom with an open door before them and not a sound anywhere. Cautiously, they padded through. They were in a set of chambers of considerable magnificence, strewn with silks and furs, with elegant furniture, sweetly scented, plants in exquisite pots of Pandahem ware. Iron-bound oaken chests, six of them, stood in a line against one wall. Crafty Kando smiled.

"Diproo the Nimble-fingered blesses us now."

The first chest revealed a mass of gems. The brilliance smote upward with the fierceness of the suns in the Ochre Limits.

At once the gang, crowing with delight, began to stuff their bags and sacks. Loot!

Silda said, "You task is only just begun. We must go on beyond the last door. There is—"

"What?" said Kando. "This is the treasure. We will fill our sacks and be gone. We shall be rich for the rest of our lives!"

"But—"

"Oh, no, my lady. You have shown us the treasure as you promised. We go not a step farther."

Chapter Sixteen

"Kill me now and have done!"

Vodun Alloran, King of Southwest Vallia, sat on the chair in the corner gazing upon Arachna's bed of offering and of prophecy, and brooded.

The four Katra Curses of his new Kataki friends take it! The Mantissae in the room sensed his mood. They stood silently. Perhaps they couldn't understand why the king was so sullen and enraged when he had taken up into his hand this great prize.

Well, ran the savage thoughts of Alloran, they were just stupid Kataki women, ugly as sin, doing as they were told. What could they know of the greater diplomacy of the outside world? Two items of news, one on the heels of the other, had shaken him far more than he cared for. By Takroti! Things looked black. The great force of mercenaries he'd expected from North Pandhahem were not coming. Their fleet had burned, and they'd got down to knocking hell out of their next-door neighbors. And, on top of that, a messenger brought news from his spies that a tremendous reinforcement fleet had arrived in the battle area along the border of Ovvend and Kaldi. That fleet was commanded by many famous kampeons, and with it flew King Jaidur and Queen Lildra of Hyrklana. At a stroke, Alloran had been deprived of an army and been faced with a fresh one.

No wonder he ground his teeth. Yet—yet! He had this whipper-snapper Prince Drak. Had him! He'd ask Arachna the questions and put Drak to her so that she could not complain that her sacrificial victim was not puissant enough. No, by the Triple Tails of Targ the Untouchable!

His bitter thoughts twined on. This King of Hyrklana, now. He was Drak's youngest brother. Yet he'd been made a king, all right, with all the huzzas. Alloran had had to fight for his kingdom.

He'd set off from Vondium to regain control of his province of Kaldi and he'd been given the Fifth Army by the emperor, and a miserable lot they'd turned out to be. He'd had to recruit himself to make up the desertions. And he'd paid good red gold for the paktuns, so that, in one way, the very worst news he'd received, a deadly body blow, was to learn Zankov was dead.

Just how Zankov got hold of the gold didn't concern Alloran. Bleakly, he stared into the future, and he flinched white-faced from what he saw.

But—but, he'd have the answers when Arachna

took her sacrifice and prophesied! Then he would know what to do . . .

"What are we waiting for?" he rasped out. "Is that bastard Drak proving troublesome?"

"No, majister," said a Mantissa. "He has been kept drugged. Listen! I hear Arachna now."

Moments later the procession entered the room. Alloran, savage, bitter, stared eagerly, desperate for the ceremony to progress so that he would know what to do. He'd have to look away at the moment of revealment; but that made no difference. Arachna—ah! All his hopes now reposed in her and her mystic powers.

One of the baby werstings decided to act as a wersting should act. He leaped forward with his babyish snarl, all yellow teeth and dripping saliva, and was hauled up in an undignified tumble by the silver lead. The giant Womox shouldering his axe moved a little away; he might be stupid, he wasn't silly enough not to know that a wersting like any hunting dog could give him a nasty bite. The Fristle fifi hauled in the dog and decorum was restored.

Clad in her swathing blue silk cloak with the mask drawn across the face, Arachna was assisted onto the bed. The liquid gleam like oil on water within the eyeslits gave Alloran a fresh upsurge of hope. Surely, this powerful sorceress *must* know the answers to his problems.

The silver gong sent out its trembling notes. The Mantissa replaced the padded hammer before returning to her place beside the bed. The second door opened sweeping the blue hangings aside and four Mantissae brought in the bound and naked form of Drak.

The questions were asked, the answers given, and then, almost gobbling in his eagerness and anxiety verging on panic, Alloran asked what he must do.

Arachna threw the cloak wide.

Alloran turned his head aside.

As though he looked through a glass where milk drained away in streaks of obscuration, Drak tried to see what was going on. His head hurt. By Zair! His head felt like the top of a volcano. He could clearly recall the girl in the white shawl saying the queen wished to see him urgently. Then what had happened? Had he heard a chink of steel? He was sure he could remember the wind in his face, and the feel of an airboat under him. Where in the name of Beng Raindrek was he now?

His vision began to clear. His wrists were bound at his back. He could see a bed. On the bed. . . . He felt lust shoot through him like melting snow in spring. The girl reminded him of someone—Queen Lush? Yes, there was much of the queen in this beauty. And—Silda. Silda whom he had seen half-naked and bloodied and fighting like a zhantilla for his life.

Whoever she was, she was his. He struggled against the bonds at his wrists. He panted, staring, making gobbling sounds, and saliva speckled his lips and ran down his chin.

The Mantissa with the knife stepped forward to slash away the hampering bonds.

* * *

"Listen," said Silda, holding tightly within herself the screaming impatience she felt at these oafish villains. "The man I love is held here. In return for the treasure you promised to help me—"

"We promised nothing, my lady. I give you thanks; but we take the gems and depart."

"You, Kando," said Lon, hearing what Lyss the Lone said and knowing that had been there all the time, and knowing, too, it made no difference to him. "You, Kando, are a faithless cramph, and no friend of mine!"

"You'll think differently when we are safe away with the treasure."

Fraipur held the heavy knife in his right hand and the wisp of straw in his left. He felt, he distinctly felt, the straw twitch.

The knife was a lethal enough weapon, something like a single-edged kalider. Yet the wizard knew that the straw was immeasurably the more powerful weapon. He lifted it, turning to the gang who were prising open the next chests.

"You will do as the lady commands. We must hurry. Follow me."

Without waiting to see their reactions or if they followed, Fraipur marched toward a blue-swathed door in the far wall. Instantly, Lon the Knees was up with him. Silda cast a look at the thieves. Kando dropped his sack of loot. He drew his knife. The others whipped out their weapons and crowded up. With Silda leading they hurried after Fraipur and Lon. The blue-covered door swung open. The little husk of straw in Fraipur's hand appeared to burn into his fingers. He saw. Understanding of what was going on sleeted over him like a lightning bolt.

"Lon!" he said in a firm hard voice that made the animal-handler jump. "On the bed. Throw your knife."

Silda barged in. She saw. She felt the bile in her, the scarlet rage, the horror—and the pain and agony and love. Lon threw. At the last, Arachna must have realized, her powers shrieking a warning. But Fraipur knew that he wielded occult magics superior, frighteningly superior. Lon's knife flew.

Alloran switched around, startled, and his hand reached for his sword hilt. The Mantissae remained fast. Their normal expectation of being told what to do checked them for those few vital heartbeats—those heartbeats that measured out the time in which the heart of Arachna ceased to beat.

Everyone was held and gripped. They stared at the bed. The knife hilt protruded from the rib cage. The body shriveled into a grayish-black leathery carapace. The gorgeous glowing face of unutterable apim beauty flowed and melted and sloughed into the low-browed, tangled-lock face of a female Kataki with the snaggle-teeth and wide-spaced eyes, narrow, cold and hostile. And yet—and yet about that face and body clung tantalizing hints of another strain. The grayish skin glinted as it were with a golden pigment imperfectly matched, the face in its bone structure might have elements of a nobility entirely foreign to a Kataki, male or female.

The long flexible whiptail tremored, rippling its entire length down the bed. The hand, the left hand at the top of the tail, flexed, opening and closing, and flopped back, cupped and still.

Thinking of Korero the Shield, the emperor's shield bearer, a golden Kildoi with just such a powerful tail hand, Silda guessed at the truth. Arachna was the fruit of a miscegenation of Kataki and Kildoi. The quick and immediate stab of sympathy for her passed Silda and left her with the hollow feeling that the fates are unjust to all seeming, and unfitted to rule the destinies of frail humankind.

Still, Arachna need not have turned her arts into the evil ways she had. Sympathy existed. That was all. More sympathy, Silda felt, was owed Arachna's mother. . . .

With wild shrieks of abandonment and despair the Mantissae leaped into action. Their bladed whiptails sliced up. Daggers glittered. Kando's gang recoiled and then, under the thrall of sorcery or because they saw there was no other way for it, they fought.

Silda ran to Drak. He turned, dazed, shaking, the sweat starting out all over his body. Alloran looked on from his chair, the sword in his fist, and he did nothing.

"Silda . . . ?"

"Drak. Here—" With efficient hands, Silda ripped the blue silk cloak away from the shriveled body of Arachna, swathed it about Drak.

She made him sit on the edge of the bed. He stopped shaking. He looked up.

"I suppose you'll tell me. But first there must be things to be done urgently . . ."

"Plenty. Alloran, for a start."

"Alloran?"

Drak didn't know what the hell had been going on; but it didn't take a genius to guess at most of it. Damned sorcery! He swiveled himself about and so looked on King Vodun Alloran.

The man still sat, gripping his sword. The sweat on his forehead glistened thickly, more profuse than the sweat upon Drak. He shook. The sword splintered lights into the overheated air of the chamber where Kando's gang fought the Mantissae. Silda felt perfectly content to leave all that physical exertion to them. After all, that was what she'd taken all this trouble to bring them here for, wasn't it?

Drak stood up. His left hand clasped the silk cloak. He stretched out his right hand.

"Silda. Lend me your sword."

Silda gave him the drexer.

Drak, sword in hand, advanced and planted himself before Alloran.

"Before you die, Alloran, you must know—"

Alloran interrupted.

"Majister! I *do* know. I *know*! Kill me and have done. I deserve only a contemptible death." He threw his sword onto the carpets.

Suddenly and bewilderingly unsure, Drak stared at this man, this traitor, who had caused so many deaths. There were meanings here that, on the surface were plain enough, and yet whose hidden truths might be twisted in ways that would make a mockery of justice.

Fraipur moved forward, avoiding a Mantissa who fell down choking her life blood out. Long Nath turned for the next one, gripped by a hatred so profound he could not resist it. Fraipur, in his turn, studied Alloran.

"Yes, San Fraipur," said Alloran in a voice hoarse and low. "I owe you the deepest apologies. I wronged you. I feel the shame, for you have been loyal to my father and to me, and I treated you. . . ." He shuddered. "Slay me, San, and rid the world of baseness."

The straw twitched like a grasshopper.

"How can you be blamed for actions forced on you by another? Arachna bewitched you. Now she is dead, you are your own man again."

"I know. I am in torment for what I have done—"

"What Arachna has done."

Fascinated—and repelled—Silda kept silent. She could see what Fraipur was talking about and appreciated the justice of it. Just that, after all the bloodshed. . . .

Drak drew a breath. What had happened had happened. He'd digest the details in time. Right now he had the winning of this damn war and the clearing of the whole of Southwest Vallia in his hands. He was not going to let an opportunity like that slip by, no, by Vox!

Chapter Seventeen

What chanced at the Villa of Poppies

That time in Southwest Vallia became known as the Hyr Kataki Jikai.

The ordinary folk just did not like Katakis. The Whiptails made their living through all the activities of slaving. For a person unfortunate enough to be taken up as a slave the world might just as well have ended. Slaves called slavemasters and slavers greeshes, a contraction in the Kregish of kleesh and grak. Kleesh, a word of so insulting a connotation it could drive a man into a frenzy of rage, and grak, that evil word meaning work, run, slave until you die beaten by the lash, added together gave vent to much of the feeling ordinary folk liable to be taken up as slave could express only in words.

The Great Kataki Hunt swept through the countryside.

There was little the Prince Majister could have done to prevent the outburst even had he wished to do anything to halt the execution of justice.

San Fraipur, restored to his green hooded robe and golden belt with rapier and main gauche, saw a little more. He spoke seriously to Drak as they took wine in an inner room of the villa given over to Drak's use.

"The people detest Katakis; but many of them do not object to owning slaves."

"My views on that are known."

"It will not be easy."

Drak sipped and said moodily, "What is?"

Silda had taken herself off the very day after the fraught happenings in Vodun Alloran's villa. She had been called away by the Sisters of the Rose, of course. How could a fellow who would one day be emperor have an empress continually going gallivanting off like this? He thought of his mother, and sighed, knowing that she had had to put up with his father's continuous absences. Queen Lush, on the other hand. . . . Well, she had arrived in great state and with enormous pomp and circumstance.

His brother, Jaidur, had changed considerably since Drak had danced at his wedding away down south in the island kingdom of Hyrklana. His wife, the queen, had gone home because of the expected happy event. Lildra didn't go chasing off over the world, did she?

Like a stage demon, Jaidur came in at that moment demanding wine. Yes, he had changed from the harum-scarum reckless rascal who'd hated the whole world and not really known why.

Since his reconciliation with their father, and his gaining the crown of Hyrklana, he had settled down to responsible government. Now he was due for a family, and more than likely it would be twins. The puncture ladies were confident.

There was going to be a whole new generation festering about under Drak's feet soon. Didi, the daughter of his sister Velia and Rog Gafard, was a grown woman now, of an age with his youngest sister, Velia. What, wondered Drak, did young Didi make of having an aunt with the same name as her dead mother?

"I saw Queen Lush in her palanquin as I rode over," announced Jaidur.

"Yes?"

"Very grand. Had to shade my eyes against her jewelry. She was heading this way, brother."

"Oh."

"Queen Lushfymi," said Fraipur in a surprisingly prim way, "is a most remarkable woman. She does have some powers of thaumaturgy, I believe, or so I have heard, though they have not been vouchsafed me."

Drak stood up and emptied his goblet.

"Think I'll take a stroll to see Alloran. I'm not absolutely decided yet. Hang him, banish him, let him take up an appointment in the army, or restore his kovnate of Kaldi to him."

Fraipur's hot feelings of anger against the kov had passed. He did say: "When the kov was under the spell of that vile woman, he had a way of deciding knotty problems."

"An old Kataki custom," said Jaidur when

Fraipur explained about the fighting men apportioned a decision each, the winner deciding. "Saw it in the Eye of the World."

"Ah!" said Drak, memories boiling up.

"Mind you," went on Jaidur, "there was a Kataki lord, feller called Rukker, when I was Vax Neemusjid, well, he, I think, had the faintest spark of humanity about him. Faint, mind, and I'd not like to meet him when he discovered he'd stolen rocks instead of our gold. Ha!"*

Drak started for the door. He thrust thoughts of the inner sea of Turismond, the Eye of the World, from him. That was where he and his brothers had received a great deal of their education. The Krozairs of Zy disciplined lads well and fairly and made men of repute out of them. As a man of repute he was scuttling off with a feeble excuse instead of waiting to greet Queen Lushfymi. What a coil!

"I'm with you, Drak," said Jaidur, finishing his wine.

Fraipur stood up, and at once, as a prince, Drak said: "You are welcome, San."

"Thank you, majister—I beg your pardon, jis."

Majis was the correct familiar diminutive for emperors, kings and princes. The little word jis, which meant "sir" was coming into general use.

They went out by a side door and the sentry slammed himself up to attention. Under the lights of the Twins, the two second moons of Kregen

*see *Krozair of Kregen*, Dray Prescot #14.—A.B.A.

eternally orbiting each other as they orbited the planet, they walked across to the outer gate in the wall where the sentry here slammed herself up to attention as rigid as her comrade at the door. Drak acknowledged and the three men walked along the street toward the villa where Alloran was now quartered. It was not the same one. That still had not been named, and now never would be, by Alloran. He was quartered now in the Villa of Poppies, with a reasonable staff to attend him.

The sentries here, all Drak's people, were pleased to see him. A few moments conversation with them ended as Drak, answering the question on all their lips, said: "I give thanks to the Invisible Twins made manifest in Opaz that Endru and Carlotta are out of danger and mend well. The news has just reached me."

"Hal, jis!" they said, pleased that their comrade Jiktar and the Jikai Vuvushi were alive.

Going into the Villa of Poppies, Drak reflected that his father often used to say that while he despaired of these folk who would thrust their bodies between him and danger, making a man feel small in the sight of Zair, it remained still a marvel and a warming wonder.

A great deal had occurred since the bandy little fellow—Lon the Knees—had given Arachna her quietus. His brother had flown in with a tremendous force of skyships, thirsting to smash the enemies of Vallia. Alloran, shaken to his foundations, had given orders to his own forces to cooperate to the full with the Prince Majister.

The mercenaries were continued on the payroll until they could be repatriated. Silda's father, Kov Seg Segutorio, had left the aerial armada to fly direct to Vondium. He had a new bride with him. Perhaps, considered Drak, going into the hallway leading to the apartments Alloran used as his withdrawing room, Silda had gone to Vondium. Tricky business, that, meeting a new stepmother. Silda's mother, Thelda, had been lost in the Time of Troubles, a sad story.

Alloran rested in a limbo at the moment, for his future was undecided, and he was now addressed as koter, the simple way of addressing a Vallian gentleman. Drak was well aware that the final decision would rest with the emperor, together with the Lord Farris and the Presidio. Paktuns could be repatriated; but the position of those native Vallians who had sided with Alloran in his treacherous revolt was different. Drak fancied that the fate of Alloran would decide the fate of his adherents. Many, of course, had already run off, sensible people.

Well, not necessarily so sensible. That was a shaming thought if carried through to its conclusion. He halted as a Khibil guard first snapped to attention and then, putting his fist onto the door handle, opened the door for the prince.

The apartments were comfortably furnished and Drak had given orders that Alloran was to be treated correctly and his necessary wants attended to politely. A little Fristle fifi, her fur of that silvery dove gray that enchanted in a fashion quite different from the golden Fristles, sat sprawled in a gilt-legged chair sobbing her heart out. The maroon and gray ribbon shook as she shuddered with each agonized wail.

Three strides took Drak to her. He bent.

Through her despair, she heard him and looked up. She had not been crying long; very soon her pretty face would be a raw wreck.

"What ails you, fifi?"

"The kov—" she managed to choke out. She pointed to the inner door.

At once, Drak understood.

"Jaidur! Fraipur! Smash that door down!"

Drak didn't even bother to check to see if it was locked. It would be. He started in on the panels with his drexer, his brother joined him, and Fraipur began to work his dagger into the crevices around the lock. If they understood or not, Drak didn't know or care; but at the urgency of his manner they set to. The door splintered and burst in.

Drak sprang into the room.

From a hook a rope drew down, taut and spinning, and in the loop the neck of Vodun Alloran was clenched fast. The chair lay tumbled on its side.

With the rush of a maniac Drak hurtled across the carpet, knocked a table over, sending a vase of flowers flying, slashed the rope asunder with his sword.

Jaidur, leaping like a leem, caught the falling body in his arms and lowered Alloran to the carpet. Fraipur bent and cut the rope free.

Alloran's eyes were closed, his face drawn, haggard with agony. The weal on his neck still glowed red.

"Pump his arms!" commanded Drak. He bellowed outside, "Send for the needlemen! *Bratch*!"

Not content, he ran across to the door. The girl was just standing up, unsteadily. Drak eyed her. "Run for the needleman, fifi! *Run!*"

Jaidur called out: "He's breathing."

"Thank Opaz!"

Still not content, for the little Fristle fifi had clearly been in a terrible state, Drak ran out after her to the doorway. He caught a glimpse of her silvery-gray fur as she raced toward the gateway. She was screaming. A guard rushed in, halberd up, looking ugly.

"The needleman!" bellowed Drak. "Bring him in here instantly! Run!"

"Quidang!"

After that all Drak could do was let Fraipur get on with doing what he could to revive Alloran, and then wait as the needleman, apprised of the urgency of the situation and yet unknowing what the exact emergency might be, rushed in and, seeing what his duty was, set to.

Alloran had not dangled there overlong. He would survive.

"The gray ones smiled on him, jis. I will just stick him a trifle. . . ." Here the needleman deftly inserted half a dozen acupuncture needles to take away any pain. "He'll live."

Drak sighed with relief. Close. That had been closer than he liked. Had Vodun Alloran died before any decision had been reached, the news would have sounded most ugly in the ears of the world. Damned ugly. The Prince Majister, folk would say, had had the kov put out of the way. . . .

"Place a guard on him," Drak told the cadade, and the guard commander nodded, understanding.

"He won't get a chance to do it again, jis."

"Make it so."

A few days later when Alloran had completely recovered, he sent word that he craved an audience with the Prince Majister. Drak happened to be taking a bur or two off from the pressing business of organizing the multifarious items necessary, and was playing a game of Jikaida with his brother. The board was filled with the ranks and columns of marching figures, all exquisitely carved and painted.

"H'm," said Jaidur, capturing a Jiktar, and cupping the piece in his fist. "I'll warrant Alloran is sweating blood right now."

"Your Eleventh Fleet—"

"Not mine. It is the Eleventh Fleet of the Vallian Air Service. I am merely the King of Hyrklana. Kapt Thando runs the Eleventh." He reached for the silver dish of greeps, slender, bright green shoots that must be cooked expertly and with precision as to temperature and duration to bring out the flavor. "What of them?"

"We sent a fast flier to Vondium with the news and have had no reply."

"That does not worry me. There has been a delay. That is all."

"Until I know what Farris and the Presidio decide, I do not particularly wish to see Alloran."

"Then," said Jaidur with a flash of his old reckless ways, "make him wait. Let him sweat some more blood."

"I suppose so. It is cruel—"

"Life is."

As though at random, although to Jaidur it was no non sequitur, he added, "I was sorry to miss Silda."

"She would joy to see you."

"Aye. I'll tell you, big brother, there was a time when if you had not been around I would have—well, Silda is Silda. When I met my Lildra it happened, as they say, as though we were shafted by the same bolt of lightning."

"I am happy for you."

"Of course! I am married and a king. Brother Zeg is married and a king out in Zandikar. Now Uncle Seg is married again—and a king. You limp along, brother, you limp along like a leem with but five legs."

Drak shifted uncomfortably in his chair.

"If I married Queen Lushfymi, then I might be King of Lome—"

"If!"

Drak felt surprise at the scornful, scoffing tone.

"She is a most remarkable woman, and I feel a very real attachment to her."

Like his twin sister, Dayra, Jaidur had no hesitation in rushing recklessly on, not caring for his brother's finer feelings, knowing them to be misguided in this instance.

"You marry that one, Drak, and you'll regret it. There is only one girl for you—"

"Who is never here. Who has no iea of what being a queen or empress entails!"

"You benighted onker!" quoth Jaidur, disgustedly.

Drak switched about and changed the subject in a marked way. "We have not fought since we were children in Esser Rarioch. Now, as to Alloran. My vote in the Presidio is for clemency. The poor devil was engulfed in sorcery. If I do not hear soon I shall make the decision—"

"Pardon him?"

"More than that. Give him back his estates and his title. His treachery was not of his volition."

"That is sooth. And we have fought—in Zy, when the Krozairs tested us—"

"That was without malice."

"Ah!"

Swinging away from the Jikaida board upon the table and standing up with a jerky, irritable gesture of his fist, Drak burst out, "By Zair! I wish I knew where Silda was now!"

Chapter Eighteen

Queen Lush—heroine

Not all the mercenaries hired by Vodun Alloran quietly accepted the needle and agreed to repatriation.

Leone Starhammer reined in and looked down on the village cupped in its little valley. It still burned. The black smoke hung greasily above collapsed roofs and fallen walls. Corpses lay about in grotesque contortions.

"The bastards have been through here, and recently," said Leone. She turned to Queen Lushfymi who rode at her stirrup.

"Then they cannot be far off," said the queen.

"May the Gross Armipand rot 'em." Leone lifted her gloved hand. "I'll get the girls moving. We'll have these Pandrite-forsaken cramphs—"

"You will use the rest of the brigade, Leone?"

A regiment of zorcabows and a regiment of zorca lancers had been placed at Leone's disposal. But they were male regiments. She sniffed.

"Only if we have to—"

"I think it would be wise."

"Yes, majestrix."

They were near enough to Rashumsmot, in all conscience. The paktuns were pillaging their way to the next port of call where they'd no doubt burn and slay and loot before seizing the ships there. That Queen Lushfymi, who had chosen to ride out with her bodyguard regiment, chanced to be the one to stumble on this band of paktuns meant in her eyes that she had been chosen by Pandrite to effect their destruction. There was no hope of taking them into her employ—not now, not with Drak and his views hovering. If only. . . . Well, that was all gone, smoke blown with the wind. . . .

As the brigade moved forward with scouts out ahead she reflected despondently and with a panic threatening to erupt, a panic she kept firmly battened down, that she just had to get Drak to speak soon. She was not growing any younger. Oh, yes, her arts kept her beauty intact and she'd not age for many and many a season yet. But she felt the passing of time, felt it cruelly.

Her spies reported that the common folk adored her. Most of them would welcome a marriage that would join the powerful Empire of Vallia with a wealthy country of Pandahem. Old enmities could be forgotten. The future looked bright.

And she, Lushfymi, would be Empress of Vallia!

She would have to have a least one child. Well, that was a sacrifice she was willing to make.

She'd pay that price and as soon as the brat

was born, or the twins,—for they were regarded as bringing good luck on Kregen—he or she could be taken off by the wet-nurses and she need never see it again except at formal functions. She wasn't prepared to risk losing her figure, no, by Pandrite!

Of course she would love her child. She did not get on with children; but her own would surely be different. Just look at the deplorable family life of the emperor!

She'd make sure Drak toed the line, that was for certain.

The scouts had spotted the mercenaries now and Leone's trumpeters pealed out orders. The brigade shook out. They were by a fraction just under a thousand strong, for they'd taken losses in the campaign and the crossing to Rahartdrin had not been easy. The paktuns, Leone estimated, numbered four or five hundred.

"Smash them," said the queen. "No prisoners."

Leone began to give orders concerning the girls to stick by the queen as the charge went in, when Lushfymi interrupted. She spoke tartly.

"No, Leone! I shall ride with you and the regiment this day."

"But—majestrix!"

"Don't argue, Leone. The paktuns do not stand a chance against us. There is no danger."

Privately, Leone told a couple of hefty Deldars to stay one each side of the queen and not to leave her no matter what.

"And drag her zorca off out of it if it turns nasty."

"Quidang!"

Leone Starhammer knew what she was about. The paktuns had only about a hundred mounted with them, and she guessed the queen dismissed the footsoldiers as a mere trifle. People got killed making foolish mistakes like that. Leone organized the attack properly, and did not take any more chances than any commander must take. The zorcabows moved forward, shooting, followed by the lancers. The bodyguard regiment, QLJV, struck in from the flank.

The result was not in doubt.

The smells were, as usual, offensive, the screams distressing. No one liked to see a zorca writhing with a dart through that supple flank. The paktuns fought for their lives, and then broke. As a wave surges up the shingle the brigide roared in and completed the rout.

A last despairing shot from a line of crossbowmen before they threw down their weapons and ran soared from the routing mass. One bolt struck Queen Lushfymi in the side. She did not fall from the saddle because the Deldars grabbed her.

Horrified, Leone shrieked for the puncture ladies.

Red blood oozed only a little, a very little, around the cruel iron barb embedded in Queen Lushfymi's soft side.

"Look, Milsi my dear," said Delia, Empress of Vallia, "when you bring your knee up you must bring it up with force sufficient to drive a man's insides up past his breastbone. Nothing else will do."

"Yes, Delia," said Milsi.

"And," said Silda, "it is wise to kick him as he falls down."

"I understand the rapier well enough," said Milsi, Queen Mab of Croxdrin. "But this throwing people about and twisting their arms and legs, and hitting them so that—"

"So that they do not give you any further trouble."

"Yes, Delia."

A tremendous crash shook the rafters on the opposite side of the salle, and the three women turned to watch, smiling, as the pile of girls there sorted themselves out. They'd been indulging in a free-for-all, and the tangle of arms and legs looked like knitting after a chavnik had played with it. Here in Lancival the only courtesies and privileges of rank existed in the structure of the Sisters of the Rose, so that Milsi, as a novice initiate, could forget she was a queen.

"You're coming along splendidly, stepmother," said Silda, and her light laugh told Milsi that the understanding between them was ripening in its own good time into affection. Neither woman wished to rush this totally important relationship.

"I am glad to hear it, stepdaughter. This Hikvar is an art I may learn. But the Grakvar!" Milsi gave a slight shudder. "Slashing a thick black whip about! That is bad enough, Opaz knows. But when I consider the Jikvar—well, I am lost for words to explain my feelings. They—"

"Not all Sisters of the Rose go through Lancival, Milsi," interrupted Delia. "Your feelings do you credit. If I do not sound too stupidly pompous, we in the SOR bear a heavy responsibility with the burden of the Jikvar upon our Order. There—am I babbling, Silda dear?"

"In no way, Delia. I did not have to snatch my claw from the knapsack, a makeshift jikvarpam, down in Rashumsmot. But—" here she turned to look hard at Milsi "—but had the necessity arisen, there would have been a number of evil folk without faces down there."

"Evil doers were sent swimming in the Kazzchun River in Croxdrin," said Milsi. "I suppose the swiftness and degree of justice may vary; the intention remains the same."

A girl clad in white leathers entered the salle. She moved with a brisk grace, her color up, her head high. Rapier and main gauche swung at her side, the jikvarpam with its red stitching neatly nestling by her hip. Straight to Delia she marched, then halted and gave the slightest tilt of her head in respectful greeting.

"FarilSheon, Delia. News."

"SheonFaril, Yzobel. Tell us."

"Queen Lush has been sorely wounded. A crossbow bolt in the side. The puncture ladies give her a fifty-fifty chance. The Prince Majister is distraught—"

"By the hairy black warts and suppurating nose of my husband's famous Makki Grodno!" Delia saw it all, saw it all in a flash, and was appalled and angry, venomously angry.

"I'll go—" said Silda.

"Of course, my dear. Opaz alone knows what mischief will chance now." But Delia knew that Silda, too, had grasped the implications and possible consequences of this disastrous news.

Milsi said, "Seg is up in Balkan now and wants me to join him. Silda, if you want me, I'll come with you."

Impulsively, Silda stretched out her hand.

"Please—Milsi—"

"That's settled, then," broke in Delia. "Yzobel—organize a fast flier, the swiftest voller we have."

"Quidang!"

"I know that stubborn, upright, sober son of mine." Delia started off for the changing rooms. "If we women cannot fashion a scheme of honor in this, then he'll deserve to be lumbered with Queen Lush, by Vox, he will!"

With which tangled sentiment, Delia led them in their headlong flight down to Rahartdrin.

Yolande the Gregarian looked in the pottery dish upon the side shelf so many times a day she lost count. The water in the dish, of an odd silvery metallic hue, just sat there, doing nothing, just plain damned water.

"You're wasting your time," Crafty Kando told her. He had accepted the needle, as they say on Kregen, and went on with his life in the old ruffianly way.

"What went—somewhere—Kando, can come back."

"Not in this life, Yolande, no by Diproo the

Nimble-fingered. The witch is dead. Her gems vanished with her. That is just plain water."

"All the same, I'll keep the water. You never know. . . ."

"How I wish I'd pocketed some of the gold! That might have remained gold instead of sorcerously vanishing—"

"You can't blame the lady Lyss the Lone. She did warn us—"

"Oh, aye! And we were used, Yolande, used. The only good thing to come out of this affair is the death of Ortyg the Kaktu and his cronies."

"They'll set the Ice Floes a-rocking."

"Aye, by Beng Brorgal!"

When Lon the Knees came in, Yolande had put on a clean dress, fluffed up her hair, and wore a nice scent.

Lon flinched back as he entered. For a moment he though a powcy had perfumed the room before he'd died and rotted instantly.

"Lahal, all," he said, and made play with a vivid green and yellow kerchief.

"Lon!" beamed Yolande, almost squirming with pleasure, desire and female intentions. "Come in. Wine?"

He sat down and accepted the wine. Yolande was about to open the proceedings on her own account, when Kando said: "Is there any more news on the queen's condition? You ought to hear all the gossip at the prince's stables."

"She still lives." Lon sipped. "They say she is so stuck with acupuncture needles a hedgehog would look bald."

Yolande stood up and went across to look in the pottery dish. The water remained water. On the way back she took the opportunity to pass by Lon's chair and put a hand on his shoulder. Lon felt the hand of doom. He remained very still. The perfume overwhelmed him and he flapped his kerchief as though driving away a fly.

"Lon, my dear," cooed Yolande. "Such a nice position you have now. Why, the Prince Majister of Vallia takes you on, give you a smart livery, lets you take care of his zorcas! You need a fine strong woman to look out for you now you are doing so well."

"One day, one day, I expect, Yolande. . . ."

"You oughtn't to leave it too long, you know. There are lots of conniving women who'd be only too anxious to take you on. Then they'd run you ragged, nag all day, fleece you of your cash—why, Lon, my dear, you need a proper woman to look after you."

Crafty Kando, thoroughly enjoying all this, hid his face in his tankard. It was ale for him. Lon, as the potential next husband, drank the wine.

Making a manful attempt to change the subject, Lon said: "They've been plagued dreadful over in the main island. They've had frogs fall from the sky, a plague of insects, and I did hear the dead rose—"

"I'm sure I don't wish to hear about that!" burst out Yolande, She smiled. "More wine, Lon my dear?"

Kando decided he'd better speak up now and

leave poor old Lon to fight a rearguard action when he'd gone.

"Look, Lon. I've a little scheme on tomorrow night. I could do with a couple of fast zorcas to—"

"You're not stealing my zorcas, Kando!"

"No, no, you fambly. Just borrowing."

"Well, I dunno. The prince has a fellow up there, Nath the Strict, who's his orderly. He has an eye like a gimlet."

"Well, Lon," said Kando, expansively. "He can be outwitted by an old leem-hunter like you!"

"Probably. I'll think about it. But I'm not going to act like an onker and lose my position. The prince trusts me."

"Of course! He like you. He won't mind if you borrow a couple of blood zorcas. And, Lon, I need 'em for the scheme to work. Speed, d'you see?"

"Oh, I see all right."

"Good! Then that's settled. Tomorrow night."

He stood up, said his thank yous to Yolande the Gregarian, and started for the door. Hastily, Lon stood up.

"I'll come with you, Kando. Work to do, you know."

"Oh, Lon!" exclaimed Yolande. "Surely you will stay for another cup of wine? And there is something I want to show you—"

"Thank you, Yolande; but I must get on about the prince's business. It's all go."

Almost killing himself laughing, Kando went out and Lon the Knees, a fixed smile on his face, his kerchief at the ready, fairly bolted after him. They called the remberees and fled into the night.

Yolande sighed, pursed up her lips, and then—just in case—trotted over to have another look in the pottery dish.

Chapter Nineteen

Queen Lush gives an order

Thandor the Rock bashed his right fist numbingly against his breastplate—he adhered to the old ways, did Brumbytevax Thandor Veltan ti Therfuing in saluting as other trifles—and bellowed out: "Well, jis, I've looked at 'em. They were coming along, coming along. But we'd have chewed 'em up and trompled 'em down, aye, by a Brumbyte's Elbow!"

"Come in, come in, Thandor, and sit yourself down and take a glass of wine." Drak indicated the chair across from his own, and the table between loaded with rather good wines.

The two Kapts sitting on the elongated chair, after the fashion of a sofa, left as much space as possible between them. Kapt Logan Lakelmi was well aware that he was an extremely fortunate man to be sitting here being treated politely as the commanding general of an army instead of being in a ditch somewhere with his head parted from his shoulders, or swinging in an iron cage with the birds disposing of him piece by bloody piece.

The Prince Majister had merely said, "You obeyed the orders of your lord, Kapt Logan. If there was sorcery influencing you, we cannot say. You were a traitor to Vallia. But you may keep your life. I think you will serve the empire and the Emperor of Vallia faithfully from now on."

Lakelmi had replied, "I believe, majister, that I, too, along with many other people, was ensorcelled. I regret what has passed. I shall hew to your person and pledge my loyalty to the emperor."

Even so, Kapt Enwood nal Venticar, with scarlet memories of battles and death, would take a time to get over what had passed. He was, as he was at pains to repeat whenever possible, an old Freedom Fighter from Valka. Valka, in his and other people's opinions, because of the struggles they had endured, bred the best soldiers, tacticians and strategists in all Vallia.

The third Kapt in this comfortable withdrawing room where Drak chose to be at ease while he sorted out the problems confronting him wore an ornate uniform in which the amount of blue cloth contrasted strikingly with the clothes of the others. Kapt Nath Molim, the Trylon of Polnehm, had brought no army with him from his native land. He'd voyaged aboard an argenter from Lome. He came to request the queen for assistance in her country, where turmoil had raged rife for many seasons. Like Vallia, the island of Pandahem was struggling to resume normal life after the Times of Troubles.

Nath Molim had been shattered to discover the queen sorely wounded and near death.

The people still loyal to her even after her long absence overseas were growing disheartened. They understood why she had fled away from them; now the evil people who battened on the unhappy land threatened to overwhelm the last bastions of resistance. Nath Molim hoped that the queen's great friendship with the imperial house of Vallia would produce men, arms and money for a great jikai to weep their enemies out of Lome.

"I swear to you, majister," he'd said to Drak, "as the Glorious Pandrite may judge me, that not one loyal soldier of Lome joined those armies from North Pandahem who attacked you here in Vallia. They came from Menaham, Tomboram and Iyam. Also, we have been much ravaged by the pirates from the Hoboling Islands who grow more daring every season."

"I believe you, Trylon Molim," said Drak, not yet on friendly enough terms to call the fellow Trylon* Nath.

Now, in this comfortable room when Brytevax Thandor the Rock entered, Nath Molim fidgeted with impatience and the hope and desire he could

*Trylon: rank of nobility below Vad and above Strom. —A.B.A.

persuade these Vallians to help him with men and treasure.

The detailed inspection carried out convinced Thandor the Rock that Alloran would in the near future have created a halfway decent Phalanx; he had not reached that stage yet. All the same, it was thankful that Thandor's three Kerchuris had not had to fight the two of Alloran's. The Rock valued his brumbytes. . . .

Comments were made about the various armies and the conversation remained exquisitely polite. Drak was worried sick about Queen Lush; but he could still find a lurking amusement in the way in which these men waltzed around each other. This was a kind of watershed. Anything could happen. This Molim fellow, now. He was quite young, smart, with a sharpness to him, a cutting edge, a fellow out for Number One all the time. There was one elegant solution that Drak fancied his father might even enjoy.

"Trylon Molim," he said, waiting for a pause in the conversation. "There are many paktuns awaiting repatriation. Many of them are from Pandahem. I think it possible I could convince the emperor and the Presidio to find the gold to pay them. They would fight for the queen in Lome and free the country for her. I do not promise, mind. But I believe this to be equitable." He was about to add that he owed the queen a great deal; he did not.

"Majister! This is just the news I was hoping for."

Kapt Logan Lakelmi, anxious to please, said:

"Give me the word, jis, and I will take my army to Lome."

"That must await the decision from Vondium."

"Yes, jis."

Drak wasn't at all sure he relished the idea. It held murky possibilities for the future.

Through the sensible arrangement of the two armies for forage and supplies, the men were now spread out over a considerable area. Here in Rashumsmot lay only the bodyguard regiments with a few ancillaries for support. At least, Lakelmi's plan would take care of his army. . . . Alloran's forces on the mainland, commanded by the Kataki Twins, had collapsed. They would provide strength for Kapt Lakelmi. As for the two Katakis, they had disappeared with their Whiptail followers.

Drak glanced over at the wall by the door where his great Krozair longsword hung. Why didn't he just take all these decisions himself? His father had once told him in that gruff way: "You do not walk in my shadow, my lad, or ever will if I have any say in the matter."

But it was damned hard not to feel that he did so walk in his father's shadow all the time. His father was just so bloody good at everything—well, except being civil—and he had the yrium, that magical charismatic power that bound men and women to him, made them loyal and ever-ready to follow him to death and beyond. Drak did not feel he shared that power; Silda was in no doubt that he possessed the yrium.

Faintly through that door he heard a commotion with a lot of shouting and yelling. Almost immediately Nath the Strict hurried in.

"There is a Jikai Vuvushi who says she must see you, jis, at once. Most urgent. The lads hold her—"

"Send her in!"

When Nath the Strict ran out he saw the girl had in some miraculous way freed herself from the grips of the guards and was running fleetly toward the door. At her back the bows lifted, arrows nocked and the cruel iron barbs ready to rip into her flesh.

"Hold!" bellowed Nath. "The prince will see her!"

Mandi Volanta fairly hurled herself through the open door. She took in the room of high-ranking officers, spotted the Prince Majister, skidded to a halt before him.

"Majister!" she fairly screamed out. "They are killing Leone! Leone Starhammer! Queen Lush has given orders to have her killed! Please, majister—do something!"

"Quite right and proper, too," spoke out Trylon Nath Molim into the abrupt hush. "The woman failed in her duty to protect the queen. Therefore she must die."

"Out of my way!" snarled Drak, and leaped for the door. He raked down the longsword as he ran.

Shouted orders, the stamp of booted feet, all a rush and a scurry, and at the head of a parcel of his lads he was out in the roseate glow of the Maiden with the Many Smiles. Mandi Volanta was up with him, directing him, shrieking for the men to run, you hulus, run!

Incongruously in Drak's brain as he pelted on the knowledge that the queen lived flamed. She had regained consciousness. And her first order had been to take vengeance on Leone, whom she blamed for her misfortune.

That, of course, was the way of the great ones of the world, of queens and empresses. It was not the way of the new Vallia.

His mother, the divine Empress Delia, would not countenance such an atrocity for an instant. But—that was the way of the world in which Queen Lush had been born and grown up and learned to understand and bend to her will . . .

Drak could not find it in his heart to blame the queen.

Sprawled in the entrance gate and across the courtyard and up the stairs the bodies of Jikai Vuvushis scattered. There were men amongst them, too, corpses wearing predominantly blue clothes. These were people in the retinue of Trylon Nath Molim, clearly, ever ready to obey their queen. This handiwork was perfectly normal for a queen, everyone knew that.

Leone Starhammer and her girls had barricaded themselves in the top floor of the villa and they resisted stubbornly. The fight was a bloody business. Drak roared into action at the head of a mingled mob of his bodyguards, yelling out for the Lomians to lay down their weapons or be chopped without mercy.

The business was touch and go. A few cunning

strokes from the Krozair longsword, a couple of lopped heads, and the Lomians understood. They heard what the prince shouted at them, and knew they must believe. If they did not—they were dead men.

As for Drak, he was perfectly prepared to slay all these Pandaheem. He valued Leone's girls. The Lomians were from Pandehem and had been implacable enemies of Vallia from long before Drak had been born. There was no contest of loyalties.

The odd fact did not occur to him until they were clearing up that many of Leone's Jikai Vuvushis were from Lome in Pandahem, too . . .

The smell of blood and the stink of fear were merely part of normal life after a fight. Leaving everything to be sorted out by his people, accompanied by a strong guard, Drak took himself off to see Queen Lushfymi.

He found her in the wide silken bed very much in command of herself, most of the acupuncture needles withdrawn, her face immaculately made-up, her hair a shining marvel. Those violet eyes were heavy with remembered pain. She sat up against silken pillows, and she smiled dazzlingly as he entered.

"Drak! How nice. I knew you would come to see me as soon as—but you are very quick! I have only just sent my tiring women away."

Instantly, she had him at a disadvantage, as it were bent across her knee, his backbone about to sunder.

He swallowed.

"Queen—Lushfymi. About Leone—"

"Oh, her, the stupid woman. I reposed great confidence in her, Drak. I felt affection for her. But she failed me abysmally. Forget her. Tell me all the news—"

He did not, he told himself savagely, he did not feel like a small boy being chastised.

This woman understood power and the management of that inscrutable and overwhelming commodity. She would make such an empress. The fabled Queens of Pain of ancient Loh might tremble with envy.

When he told her that he had saved Leone Starhammer she became outraged. Her face took on a menacing look that would have struck terror into the purest of her subjects.

"You had no right to interfere with my justice!"

"Lushfymi, look, that was scarcely justice—"

"Of course it was! Does the workman keep a broken tool? Does a warrior retain a worthless sword?"

"It wasn't Leone's fault—"

"Oh! So it was my fault, was it?"

"No, of course not—"

"Perhaps we had best forget this, Drak. After all, I think we must come to a conclusion soon in our relationship and you do know in what fond regard I hold you." She smoothed the silken sheet. "I am sure you thought you were acting for the best."

"Yes—"

"So let us brush aside the silly woman. If Leone lives, then she is lucky for now. Nath Molim is most anxious for us to go to Lome and drive out all these awful villains preying on my country. Between us, we can do it."

Feeling despicable, Drak took refuge in saying, "The decision must rest with the Presidio and the emperor."

"Ever since he fell through the covering of my palanquin, Drak, I have felt an affection for your father."

That wasn't quite as Drak had heard the story from his mother; he let it pass without comment. Lushfymi was a formidable woman, a queen acting perfectly within her rights, and a force of personality and character able to deal with any and every aspect of running Vallia as empress.

Lushfymi, conscious of the power she held over Drak and yet frustratingly aware that the conclusion for which she hungered appeared as far away as ever, lay back on her pillows. She smiled, a wan yet brave little smile. She knew she was beautiful, not just because everyone told her so but because she could see the evidence in her mirror day by day.

"Drak, dear, I am very tired. I am so pleased to see you, but—"

"Of course."

"Drak—kiss me before you go—please . . ."

He kissed her on the cheek and she turned her head so that her full soft lips met his. She knew all there was to know about kissing. Drak drew back, feeling the passion there. He managed a smile, and then turned and contrived to keep from stumbling as he made for the door.

By Zair! What an empress she would make! And what a wife! He could not mistake the naked passion blazing in her, and no matter how much of that was for the position of empress and how little for himself as a man, whatever she spared him would be more than enough for any man. No other woman had ever aroused so deep emotions within him, except for Silda, of course; but Silda was different.

The next day his mother, Silda, and her new stepmother, Queen Mab, flew in. They were closely followed by a second voller bringing Senator Naghan Strander, a senior and highly valued member of the Presidio, from Vondium.

The welcomes were genuine and warm, the rejoicings great. Drak found Milsi to be delightful. She, for her part, saw at once that Silda had better marry Drak quickly. The man was a splendid person; but he needed a great deal of female instruction. With Lushfymi acting as the wounded heroine of a battle, for all that the fight had been but a skirmish, Silda's light was being eclipsed.

Naghan Strander brought the decision. Alloran was to be pardoned on account of sorcery, and to be restored as Kov of Kaldi. Drak was pleased.

During the next days the mercenaries, willing to go fight for Queen Lush if they were paid, prepared to embark for Lome. The town hummed with activity. During this time there were opportunities for enjoyment, dances, routs, balls and festive occasions. Lushfymi mended apace. Silda and Milsi got on famously. And the women scrupulously made no mention of the reason for their visit, were exquisitely polite to Queen Lush, oohing and aahing at her version of the battle in which she had been wounded.

Delia, sizing up Leone Starhammer, agreed to take the Jikai Vuvushi into her personal regiment. There was no chance that Leone could serve Queen Lush again, and every chance she'd die of the attempt if she made it.

The mercenaries sailed in the fleet gathered by Alloran in his attempt to conquer the islands. Naghan Strander informed the Lomians that the Presidio had vetoed Kapt Lakelmi's plan to take his remaining forces to Lome. He would go with Alloran back to Kaldi. The large island of Womox, off the west coast, had been recaptured by Delia's Blue Mountain Boys. Vallia was being reunited. North Vallia remained to be brought back into the fold. But the Vallians were aware that they were being held in reserve against the horrendous invasions of the Shanks, fishmen from over the curve of the world, who would destroy all of Paz if they were not stopped.

News came in when the town lay quiet after all the excitements that Kovneva Katrin Rashumin had been in hiding with the wizards in their island of Fruningen. She was returning to her kovnate of Rahartdrin. Delia was overjoyed at the news, for Katrin was a trusted friend of standing. San Fraipur smiled, nodding, and said words to the effect that wizards of his home were not onkers.

One day Milsi said to her stepdaughter, "Silda,

my dear, I really do think I must join your father in Balkan. He needs me up there."

"Very well, Milsi." Silda wasn't going in for the mother style of address. "I understand. Give him my love."

Delia said, "I think my son is nerving himself for a decision. It is useless to prod him. I think, Silda, Milsi and I are doing more harm than good here."

"Delia!" burst out Silda. "That can't be true!"

"I think it is. We are clearly supporting you. We are a pressure group. Poor Queen Lush, wounded, alone, with no one to urge her suit!"

So Silda had to stand and wave them good-bye and call the remberees. What they said was true; it hurt to see them go.

To stifle off that feeling she made up her mind to go and see the person she had promised herself to go see for longer than she cared for. She tried not to be ungrateful. There was, also, the question of gold to be accounted for . . .

At this time Drak made up his mind that as soon as Queen Lush was fit to travel they'd be off back to Vondium. With Katrin Rashumin returning, and Kapt Enwood and the army here, this corner of Vallia was safe.

Naghan Strander told him that the Presidio had been divided over the fate of the traitor Alloran. The emperor had pointed out that the Prince Majister, as the man on the spot, was in the best position to judge. "They all acknowledged the truth of that, Drak. I can say I am mightily pleased at the respect they all hold you in."

So to return to Vondium should not create problems.

He could not deny that he would be pleased to see his father again. He might be an old devil; but he represented to Drak a very great deal of what life was about. His father had always been honest with him, except for these mysterious disappearances, unexplained, and he had only once ever thought with any certitude that his father had lied to him.

One day in Esser Rarioch, seasons and seasons ago, Drak had spotted a wonderful golden and scarlet hunting bird and had called out in surprise at the gorgeous raptor. His father had denied that the bird existed. Yet Drak had seen it. Of course, he'd been very young at the time, and much smoke had blown with the wind since then and he'd grown up. Maybe that had something to do with it?

He pulled on light russet hunting leathers over a shirt of linked mesh and, dressing without thinking about it, strapped on rapier and left-hand dagger. Calling for Nath the Strict he raked down the Krozair longsword, bellowing: "Nath!"

A footman, scarlet of face, hight Brindle, popped in hurriedly. "Nath has a demon in his guts, jis. Lon the Knees—"

"Send Nath my condolences. Lon the Knees will handle the zorcas." He went out quickly, feeling stifled indoors, needing a breath of fresh air. He told the sentry to alert the Hikdar in command of this day's duty squadron.

At the stables Lon was competence itself. A fine blood zorca was brought out, Stiffears, and Lon handled himself and the zorca splendidly. He assisted the prince to mount. No one could guess from his rubicund face that if the prince had turned up a glass later disaster would have befallen Lon the Knees.

Silda walked into the courtyard, over the cobbles with the wisps of straw scattered about, and saw Drak astride the zorca.

Lon faded into the shadows of the nearest box. He hadn't seen Lyss the Lone since all the excitement, and was enraptured to see her come visiting him now. He thought the prince wouldn't mind; but you had to be careful when you held a responsible position in the Prince Majister's Stables!

Silda was in a mood that sizzled like water dropped into hot fat.

"Off to see Queen Lush, I suppose?"

"I was going for a ride." The stiffness of Drak's tones made a pikeshaft look crooked. "Now you mention it, I think I will. Thank you for the suggestion."

"Oh, you are most welcome."

"The queen is wounded, you know, and—"

"Rubbish! There's nothing wrong with the fat old madam now!"

"You forget yourself!"

"I don't! But I wish I did!"

Drak, face like the base end of a marble statue, touched his spurless heels into the zorca's flanks and Stiffears bounded away. Drak and Silda, both their heads seething with half-understood anger and anguish, parted.

Lon closed his mouth.

He made a slight movement and caused just a tiny chink of sound. Instantly the sharp point of a rapier pressed against his stomach. Silda stared into the shadows.

"Lon?"

"Aye, aye, Lyss, it's me. What I can't understand is why you're still here and not lying with your body there and your head here! You spoke to the prince—"

"Forget him, the great onker! I came to see you."

Lon felt convinced that the brightness in Lyss's eyes was far greater than could be explained in any except one certain way. He swung about as the gang crept quietly into the stables. They had waited until the prince left. Now Crafty Kando, looking at Lyss, said, "We're here. And so is the lady."

At once Silda was herself again. She fixed Lon with a look. So he felt obliged to explain. Kando had borrowed the two zorcas he'd requested, and the job had been completed. Now far greater game was afoot. The whole gang required zorcas.

"He is a fat slaver, Lyss! He still has slaves out there, hidden. He has gold! Rafak is a chicken ripe for the plucking! Ride with us!"

"If this Rafak continues as a slavemaster," said Silda, "he breaks the law."

"Exactly!" crowed Lon.

"Then he should be reported to the Watch, or the Prince—"

"We don't have much truck with the Watch. And we value his gold, believing it should come to us—"

"What am I to do with you?" said Silda, thoroughly cheered up after that dismal encounter with Drak. "This sounds promising. A spot of mischief thrashing a slaver is just what I need."

Swathed in dark hooded cloaks, riding a string of the Prince Majister's blood zorcas, the gang rode out. Silda rode with them. Drak had needed to go for a ride to rid his head of cobwebs; Silda craved more than a simple ride to rid her brain of the festering agony and anguish there . . .

Lon the Knees gave up trying to puzzle out what he'd overheard. Perhaps he hadn't heard all that at all. Perhaps he'd dreamed it, hiding in the zorca stall. . . . He, too, felt that a spot of action would clear his head.

The petal shape of an airboat skimmed over the riders and swooped ahead to vanish beyond trees cloaking a rise.

Moving at a brisk pace, for there was a lot to be got through, Crafty Kando's gang with Lon the Knees and Silda Segutoria, very much Lyss the Lone, rode for the criminal hideout of the slavemaster, the Rapa Rafak the Lash.

Some time later with a great deal—but not all, by the Furnace Fires of Inshurfraz, not all!—of his ill humor jolted out of him by the ride, Drak cantered back. The duty half-squadron rode in rear, looking forward to a wet and the opportunity to relax in their various raucous, nefarious or slumbrous ways. A jurukker of the guard detailed to Queen Lush galloped frenziedly toward Drak.

"Prince! The queen! She is beset by Katakis!"

The rider skidded his zorca around, spraying dust, still bellowing.

"The queen! Assassination! Hurry, jis, hurry!"

Without hesitation Drak slammed his heels into Stiffears' flanks. The zorca leaped ahead, responding at once, and in the same instant Drak hauled up on the reins, as a figure darted from the side to stand directly before him, one hand flung aloft.

"What the hell! Out of the way—or . . ." Drak was going to say he'd run the figure over; but he saw the long plain robe, the turban toppling over one ear, and so he guessed at once, with a distinct sensation of his heart turning over and lodging in his throat. He knew, did Drak, he knew.

"Drak! Silda! The Katakis attack her and her companions believing you to be there. She is sore beset. . . . There is little time left for her. . . ."

Chapter Twenty

In which Lon the Knees witnesses the true joy

On the day Queen Lushfymi gave orders to have the captain of her bodyguard killed the girls had resisted the murderers in defense of Leone Starhammer. Since then nearly all of them had signed up with the Empress Delia. So it was that when the Katakis landed from their airboat to assassinate the queen they were met by the guard detailed by the Prince Majister to watch over the queen.

The guards sent a messenger and then barricaded themselves in the villa. No thought crossed Queen Lush's mind that this was divine retribution. She saw no connection between her perfectly logical and legal order and this inspired assassination attempt.

One of the guards said that the leader of this cut-throat bunch of Katakis was Stromich Ranjal Yasi, twin brother to Stom Rosil Yasi. Accurate archery pinned the Katakis in the grounds, and two rushes were fronted and bested. The queen was perfectly composed. Hikdar Nervil remarked that they could hold out for some time yet, but that numbers were against them.

Queen Lush said, simply: "The Prince Majister will soon be here. He would melt the Ice Floes of Sicce to be at my side."

"Assuredly, majestrix," said Nervil, seconded to Drak's PMSW from 3EYJ, and took himself off to the dangerous corner where the shrubbery grew altogether too close to the walls of the villa.

For Silda, the ride to Cottmer's Hollow knocked some of the bad humor out of her. The ride alone began to affect her. She shouldn't really have spoken to poor Drak like that; after all, he was completely deceived by Queen Lush. She'd have to make it up to him, as soon as possible. All the same, he was so stubborn! If only she could knock some sense into him as the zorca between her knees was jolting the bad temper out of her!

Crafty Kando organized the onslaught brilliantly. Silda could quite see why the gang needed zorcas; they could hit Rafak the Lash, free his slaves and steal his gold, and be back in town before anyone knew anything about it.

Rafak, his vulturine features convulsed, feathers bristling, his arrogant beak bent to one side, was not slain. The slaver with his assistants was bundled into one of the tumble-down shanties at the center of the hollow. Massy trees surrounded the place, which was gloomy and dank, and well named for Cottmer's Caverns of horrific legend.

Silda realized she would have to fend for the slaves herself. She went around freeing them, and they set up a caterwauling, running about, wringing their hands in joy, overwhelmed by the tragedy and then the release. Lon the Knees, after a single thought, joined Silda in her work.

Crafty Kando and his cronies sought the gold chests.

So it was that when the flier landed and the Kataki Strom led his people into this vengeful attack upon the man who had authored his downfall, he was not aware that the Prince Majister was not in Cottmer's Hollow. Yasi was convinced that the string of zorca riders from the prince's stables escorted the Prince Majister. Now he would exact his revenge.

Shrieking shrill Kataki war cries, the Whiptails rushed in, weapons glittering.

Silda grasped the situation in a single all-encompassing glance and dragged Lon into the shanty where Kando and his people were ripping everything to pieces in their search for gold. Crossbow bolts thudded into the walls and ripped through the mean little windows. The consternation and uproar in the hut could not be allowed in any way to influence her.

Lon saw her switch the plain knapsack forward. She dived her left hand in, and he remembered what had happened to the spinlikl when he had done just that. Then he gasped.

Silda raised her left hand high and shouted at the rabble in the shanty.

Clothing that left hand, glittering, evil and magnificent, a Claw, a thing of oiled sliding steel, of cruel razor-sharp talons, turned Silda into a true Jikai Vuvushi of the Sisters of the Rose.

"Listen to me, you famblys! Those Katakis out there—all they're after is slaves and gold—your gold! And you as slaves! They will not take me."

Her Claw struck sparks of fire from the honed talons, turning, opening and closing, evil and beautiful. . . .

She'd taken up the jikvar in the emergency quick-action grip and now as Kando's people yelled and swirled around like a disturbed ant's nest, Silda strapped up the Claw properly onto her left hand.

The opening moves from the Kataki side consisted in driving Kando's people into the shanty, of rounding up the newly released and bewildered slaves, and then of sorting out the rest. Silda reasoned out this probable course of action and then gave vent to her feelings on certain subjects.

"You refused my offer of swords. How many of you retain the spears I provided? And not a bow among us! By Vox! It's enough to make an honest Jikai Vuvushi take up knitting!"

"It's enough to make an honest thief know when to keep his station," pronounced Yolande the Gregarian, with a meaningful look at Kando. Some of the others started in slanging Kando, each other, themselves for their own stupidity, and Lon the Knees for providing the zorcas that got them into the mess. To Silda it seemed a bubble burst in her head. They made her laugh, these people and their thieving antics. Her ill-humor now had but one direction, one target. Katakis!

"If we just stay here and wait for them to attack when they are ready." She spoke in a hard, clipped fashion Lon had heard her use once before. "They'll chop us for sure. We must break for the zorcas, and ride. All of us, together."

"These walls may not be much," rapped out Kando. "But they stop the crossbow bolts. If we stay here they can't shoot us, and if they try to break in, we will chop them."

"Aye," said Lop-eared Tobi, waving his knife about. "But I'll go with Lyss the Lone. I trust her."

"I'll stay with Kando," said Ob-eye Mantig, and he showed the spear he had kept.

The others started up for and against the plans.

Keeping watch out of a crack, Lon yelped: "You'll have to make up your minds sharpish. Here they come."

Silda recognized that these folk had little hope of escaping this imbroglio. If they were not killed out of hand they'd wind up as slaves. And that fate might include her. . . .

Hissing shrieks of battle spitting from the Katakis heralded their attack that would finish off the people sheltering in the shanty. Silda swung to face the ramshackle door, Claw poised, drexer snouting, ready.

The phantom form of Deb-Lu-Quienyin, glowing with a ghostly light, faded. He had used his kharrna to project his image mile after mile across

Vallia to warn Drak. What effect this sorcery might have on his men did not concern Drak now.

Queen Lush!

Silda!

Drak did not have to make a decision.

There was no agonized despair over what he must do. He wrenched the reins about and Stiffears, unused to such summary treatment, gave a little snort of reproval. The queen must be cared for and protected, nothing less would satisfy a prince of so upright a character, so he yelled savagely at her messenger.

"Ride for the Villa of Poppies! Rouse out Kov Vodun and his men! Bring all the people you can from anywhere you can—and ride like the Agate-Winged Warriors of Hodan-Set!"

"Majister . . . ?"

But Drak was gone, heels clapped into Stiffears, slapping the zorca's rump, hurtling him on. His duty half-squadron followed, picking up speed. Hikdar Nath the Meticulous yelled across at the youngest jurukker of the squadron.

"Jurukker Vaon! Ride for the barracks, get anyone you can, dig 'em all out! Ride for Cottmer's Hollow—and, Vaon—*Bratch*!"

"Quidang, hik!"

Vaon's zorca leaped away heading for the barracks.

Drak, Prince Majister of Vallia, rode like a crazy man.

If anything happened to her! If she was killed, wounded. . . . Those Zair-benighted Whiptails were expert at man management, and women in their nets could hope only for a cruel fate to be curtailed by death. He was under no illusions. He remembered what his mother had told him, speaking in soft unhappy tones, repeating what his father had said. Once his father had sought to save Velia, the first Velia. Oh, no, real life was not like the romances of the theaters, of the puppet shows, where the valiant prince always rode to the rescue in time.*

Stiffears was now under no illusions either; he recognized the urgency in the rider on his back, and true to the pride and prowess of a bloodzorca, he responded. He stretched out into a long headlong gallop that swept him over the ground like a bird. Low in the saddle, glaring ahead, Drak forced the zorca on, and he could feel the blood in his body thumping in time to the staccato clatter of the hooves.

Very quickly they left the road and went roaring across open country, soaring up wooded slopes and pressing on across shallow streams, racing over the open heathland.

If anything happened to her, Drak promised himself in rage and useless vengeance, he would hang every Kataki sky-high, every one, no matter what, from this day on until he was sent down to the Ice Floes of Sicce to meet the Gray Ones and perhaps make his way to the sunny uplands beyond. Every last damned one. . . .

*see *Renegade of Kregen,* Dray Prescot #13.—A.B.A.

* * *

The door was smashed and hung from one hinge. They'd piled up benches and the table and fought the intruders back; but Long Nath lay coughing blood from a Whiptail's bladed steel in his guts, and Nath the Swarthy sprawled dead, his throat ripped out. Crafty Kando lunged his spear into a Kataki who screeched and fell back beside a fellow who lacked a face.

Lon the Knees had seen Lyss at work, and he shuddered even as he thrust his spear through a crack in the walls, and heard an answering yell. The Katakis attacked from all sides of the shanty, trying to break in, so the occupants had no chance to follow Lyss's plan and force their way out and away astride the prince's zorcas.

No one now questioned Silda's right to give orders and to take control of the defense of the hut. These folk recognized a professional at work. The first Kataki through with his bladed tail high ready for that twinkling downward slashing blow or that treacherous and devastatingly quick upward lunge, leaped forward, sword flashing, to seize his prey, and Silda's Claw raked and the Kataki did not scream as he fell away. Difficult to scream without a mouth, let alone a face.

The acrid stinks in the hut, the sweat and blood, all meshed to make a miasma of horror. The thieves, seeing there was nothing else for it, fought wickedly. Well led, they fronted and hurled back the first Kataki attacks. But time was against them. If the Whiptails gave up trying to take the merchandise they might fire the hut and burn them out. . . .

The table and benches groaned and slid away from the pitiful door. Three Whiptails sprang through. Kando ducked and put his spear into the last one's ribs. Of the first two, one looked—for a single heartbeat only—most stupidly at his stump of tail, the steel blade tinkling across the floor. Then the drexer investigated his inward parts and before he had time to fall, in that cunning swirling movement of the Claw his comrade gushed blood and brains and stumbled emptily back.

"They keep coming," snarled Kando, swiping sweat from his forehead. "I think, my lady Lyss, we are done for."

"Dee Sheon will aid us, Kando. We fight until we can fight no longer."

Lon stuck a Whiptail trying to bash the crack wider with an axe. He peered out. Then he swung back to shout at Silda: "They're pulling back at the rear, Lyss. I think—"

"Yes, you are right. It's one last charge into the door. After that, if we live, they'll burn us out."

The parcel of thieves prepared themselves. They would resist, they would fight back this one last time. They would not be taken up as slaves by Katakis. Silda allowed one regretful thought that she had not seen her father for far too long, and she mourned her mother. As for Drak, well, the stars had remained icily aloof. . . .

"Here come the greeshes!"

Smashing their way over the tumbled table

and benches the Katakis forced their way in. They slashed and hacked and the spears darted and stabbed in return. Silda's sword cut and thrust, and her Claw flamed brilliantly. The cunning steel talons sprayed blood. She cut down two Whiptails, and a third ripped his tail-blade across her thigh. She did not notice the sting. She brought the Claw around and rearranged his features. His blood hit Lon, who blinked, and drove on with his spear. From the back of the hut knives flew expertly.

A looped rope entangled a Kataki and as he stumbled Yolande stuck her knife into him.

As Diproo the Nimble-fingered was their witness, the thieves fought.

The force the Katakis put in was just too much. In the next few moments the thieves would be overwhelmed. Silda took a fresh grip on herself, snouted the sword up, a single glistening bar of red, slashed her Claw before her eyes. If this was the way of it, why, then, this was the way of it . . .

The Krozair longsword, among the most formidable weapons of all Kregen, simply cut through the Katakis as a reaper cuts corn. Drak ploughed through, scattering arms and legs, tumbling heads, berserk. He cut a pathway through to the smashed door, striking down without a vestige of mercy at the backs of the Whiptails trying to break in. He was a devoted instrument of destruction.

His duty half-squadron, very professional, took care of those Katakis who were rash enough to stay to contest the outcome. Drak burst his way into the hut.

He saw Silda, smeared in blood, her Claw a glistening horror, slide her sword into a Kataki and swirl the Claw around to destroy another. He chopped the remaining Katakis with swift, economical blows, coming back to his senses, using all the skill inherent in the Disciplines of the Krozairs of Zy. The last slaver fell. Drak halted, sword uplifted, staring at Silda.

"You are safe," he said, stupidly, feeling the shakes beginning. He lowered the sword and bowed his head.

Silda could say nothing. She needed to breathe.

Lon the Knees saw it all.

He had given himself up for lost, and now the prince had rescued him and the others. There would have to be some nimble explanations about those zorcas. He saw the prince drop that terrible sword. He saw Lyss the Lone drop her sword. That awful Claw-thing on her hand fell to her side. Lon saw. He saw the prince step forward and take Lyss into his arms. He heard him speak.

"Silda! Silda—a fool, I've been—"

"Hush, Drak. You are here. I am here—"

"Oh, yes!"

Lon's mouth tried to close and would not.

"And, Silda, we shall be married at once. If you will have me—?"

"There is never anyone else, ever, Drak—"

"When I heard—Deb-Lu warned me—I knew I would not want to live without you—"

"Nor I you—"

"And, Silda, my heart, we are going to be so happy the whole world of Kregen will marvel!"

"Oh, yes, Drak, my heart. Oh, very yes!"